BROKEN REBEL

BROKEN PEAK PACK
BOOK 4

BY JULES CRISARE

BROKEN PEAK PACK

Broken Hero
Broken Sage
Broken Mage
Broken Rebel
Broken Crown
Broken Witch

HIDDEN RUNAWAYS

Hidden Trouble

BLACK HILLS VENDETTA

Wolf's Retribution
Wolf's Revenge
Wolf's Reckoning *(coming to Kickstarter in 2024)*

BOX SETS

Broken Peak Pack eBook Bundle Volume 1
Broken Peak Pack eBook Bundle Volume 2
Broken Peak Pack Omnibus Collector's Edition *(Kickstarter Exclusive)*

SILVER SENTINEL NOVELS

Destined Heir
The Last Immortal Mystery Files *(coming to Kickstarter in 2023)*

SENTINELS OF THE SILVER ORB

BROKEN REBEL

BROKEN PEAK PACK
BOOK 4

BY JULES CRISARE

SILVER ORB BOOKS

BROKEN REBEL

ISBN: 978-1-948603-30-0 (pbk.)

For everyone who loves trashpandas.

PROLOGUE

A History of Shifters & the Role of the McCallisters
—from Edna McCallister's journal

IN THE beginning, when the Great Shifters took flight and ruled from the skies, the lesser shifters maintained a respectful distance, even though they were all formidable apex predators.

While the animals avoided lesser shifters, they were drawn to the Great Shifters. One animal in particular, raccoons, lived closer than the others, and the Great Shifters didn't discourage them, probably because they found the raccoons entertaining. As the years passed and the time of war drew closer, one dragon considered the traits of the raccoons, the eventual needs of the Hero, and the magic that lived within the Great Shifters, and came to a conclusion. The Great Shifters accepted their fate, but they didn't have to accept a future where lesser shifters and supernaturals were hunted to extinction by humans. The Hero would need all the help the Great Shifters could set in motion.

With that in mind, the Dragon identified some of the most cunning and industrious of the raccoons and with the assistance of the wizard they protected, sent a drop of the Dragon's magic into the chosen raccoons.

Both the wizard and the Dragon Shifter waited, but nothing happened in the first hour, day, or week. It wasn't until the next generation of kits when the Dragon's magic emerged and a new shifter entered the ranks of the lesser shifters.

A thousand years would pass before the Rebel was born, but she would carry within her the magic of the Dragon and a hint of the wizard's power as she stood next to the Hero.

CHAPTER ONE

MAGGIE slid down between the large rock and tree when the rumble of an approaching vehicle reached her ears. She shirked most Gaze duties by running to this spot in the territory. It butted up against the state park along the back and Gaze members rarely wandered back there, much preferring the populated areas closer to the temple. Someone arriving by foot was rare enough, but no one ever drove up to her hiding spot since she first found it almost fifteen years ago when she had just turned ten years old.

In case the recent visitors found her, she tucked her book inside the small hole in the tree. She kept several treasures in the tree, away from the prying eyes of the Gaze and the punishing whims of Zachery, the Gaze leader.

A mauve, yes, it was mauve, luxury sedan pulled around the front of the tree and parked a good twenty-five feet away from Maggie's hiding spot.

What the hell was *he* doing here? Zachery only traveled in the Mercedes S-Class and after he purchased one, the leaders of the other Gazes followed suit. No one leader could appear better than the others.

Martin, head enforcer for the Gaze and Zachery's right hand, jumped out from the driver's seat of the car and opened the back passenger door. Zachery climbed out of the car and immediately smoothed out the wrinkles of his blue tunic. Everyone in the Gaze wore clothes in a similar color of blue. But where his garments were made from luxury fabrics like cashmere and silk, most other Gaze members wore rough cotton or wool.

Maggie looked down at the hem of her own blue tunic, sticking out from beneath the scratchy blue wool sweater.

The sound of the trunk opening and closing, followed by the muffled wailings of a man, yanked Maggie away from worrying about the loose thread on the hem of her sweater threatening to unravel.

She should have left right away.

She shouldn't have succumbed to her curiosity and peeked through the small crevice between the rock and the tree.

If she hadn't, she wouldn't have heard Zachery telling Andy, one of the more vocal members of the Gaze, that he'd been talking out of turn and they couldn't trust him to keep quiet anymore. She also wouldn't have witnessed Martin lifting a gun and holding it under the struggling Andy's chin. She wouldn't have seen the trigger pulled or heard the gunshot. And she never would have seen Andy's, now limp, body fall to the ground.

Holllllly Shiiiiiit.

This was bad. This was so bad.

Before they caught sight, or scent of her, Maggie grabbed her book from its hidey hole and crept away from the scene of the murder as quickly as possible without making noise.

She needed to get home.

She needed to tell someone. Her dad. Her dad would know what to do. She couldn't trust her mother. The woman was too enthralled with Zachery not to turn her own daughter over to the fucker.

Once she figured she was far enough away from her secret place, that turned out to be someone else's secret place too, Maggie broke out in a run. She enjoyed running, but this wasn't like all those other times when she imagined racing towards something, anything found outside of the Gaze. This time she was running from something.

Away from discovery.

Away from punishment.

Away from death, that would likely be more welcoming than the punishment Martin doled out at Zachery's whim.

She couldn't look behind her. Looking back would mean they would catch her. So indoctrinated to the idea of Zachery knowing all, she was convinced he was aware of her presence. Even if he wasn't chasing after her, he didn't have to. Zachery knew where she was headed.

Home. To her father.

Her feet pounded harder against the ground with a fresh burst of speed. Her house was in view. A few more seconds, less than fifty more steps. Her ears listened for the sound of an approaching car, but the surrounding area was silent. Her eyes scanned the distance for any one lurking in the shadows and ready to pounce before she could break through the barrier of the doorway.

Maggie's father must have heard her approach. As soon as the rubber soles of her blue canvas shoes hit the stones of the walkway, the front door flew open.

"What's wrong?"

She sprinted inside and pushed the door closed, leaning back against it. As if her weight could stop anyone from pushing their way inside.

"Margret, what's wrong?" Her father rarely used her given name. If the hitch in his voice didn't convince her of his worry, his use of Margret instead of Maggie would have cinched it.

Now that she was as safe as she could be for the moment, Maggie didn't know where to begin. She stared at her father, opening and closing her mouth like a landed fish.

"Margret, tell me." His fingers tightened around her shoulders as he gently shook her. "Tell me what's got you in such a state?"

"Zachery…" Maggie breathed in, filling her lungs with some much needed oxygen. "Martin. Martin, he killed Andy."

Conrad Iotor closed his eyes and breathed in as deep as Maggie had a few moments before. "Did he see you?"

"No. I don't know. Maybe."

"We have to assume he knows, Maggie." Her father's fingers dug into her flesh. "You need to get out of here. It's the only way."

"We can both leave. We almost have enough saved for us, right? You'll go with me."

"No, Maggie. The bond with your mother is still present. If I leave with you now, I'll just get sick and slow us both down until…"

"No. No, Daddy, you have to come with. Zachery will kill you if you stay here."

"He can't. It would kill your mother too. Like I said, the bond hasn't faded enough yet." He straightened his spine and straightened hers as well. "Leave everything. Take the RV and go."

What? Just leave him? Maggie blinked slowly at her father. "I don't even know where to go."

"War. Drive to War and stay hidden. Zachery isn't stupid enough to risk grabbing you in public. Once in War, look for a shifter, maybe a fox or wolf, but he's old. If he's still alive, he'll help you. He's one of the MacAllisters, and they've always helped any of our kind in need."

"Raccoons?"

"Shifters. He's one of the good ones. Find him and no matter what happens, you can trust him." Conrad walked away from his daughter and into the kitchen. Ducking under the sink, he reached for the old metal coffee tin, rusted with age, hidden in the damp recesses. Somewhere in the bottom of the can, buried under the nails and screws, as ancient as the can, lurked a collection of keys that would take her to her freedom. Her father fished them free and handed them over. "Go. Quick, before Zachery or Martin gets here."

"But what about you?" Maggie wasn't worried about running, she had evaded being swept into Gaze practices by being quick. Leaving her father behind was something she had never considered when her father suggested they plan for a future outside of the Gaze. And it wasn't something she wanted to consider now.

"Don't worry about me. Once the bond with your mother breaks, I'll find you. And while we're waiting, I'll keep my head down and continue to play the oblivious idiot." Conrad reached out for Maggie and hugged her tight. "Now, go. You don't have much time."

Maggie brushed away a tear with the back of her hand and nodded at his words. If she opened her mouth, she'd cry even more. And it wouldn't be a pretty cry. It'd be an ugly cry. One of those better done in the privacy of your shower because no one needed to witness it.

She kissed her father's cheek and slipped out the back door, instead of heading out the front.

Leaving together had been part of the plan since they came up with it over eight years ago, when Maggie turned sixteen and Zachery's leer found her more often than not. Not for the first time, Maggie wished her mother had died. The bond between her parents would have snapped and it would have been hell for her father, but at least they would already be far away from the Gaze and she wouldn't be leaving him behind.

By the time she reached the storage shed with the RV, a few hours had passed. As near as she could tell, she hadn't been followed. Though not being followed didn't mean Zachery hadn't sent Martin out to intercept her. She needed to get on the road and head to War, just like her father said. And the sooner the better.

Her hands shook as she slipped the smaller key into the padlock, keeping the storage unit secure. It took three attempts before the hasp snapped free and another two tries before she pushed the door up. The front windshield of the small RV greeted her and Maggie let out a long breath.

Freedom was so close, she could taste it. Except it came with a hint of bittersweetness. In every scenario she had played out in her mind, her father accompanied her.

"Suck it up, Maggie. You don't have time to wallow. And if they don't have you, they can't use you against Dad. He might even be safer on his own."

Great. Now, she was talking to herself.

She unlocked the door into the trailer and stepped into the darkness. Dust and dampness invaded her nostrils, but she didn't have time to worry about it at the moment. Once she was away from the Gaze and far enough from the long arm of Zachery's reach, Maggie could worry about giving the RV a scouring.

First things first. Get out of her Gaze uniform. If she dressed like the humans she hoped to hide amongst, she had a better chance of getting away before someone spotted her. Her father and she had bought some old clothes at a thrift store. Just some jeans and shirts, but they'd do. She stripped off the blue clothing and left it in a pile on the floor. She wanted to throw it out, but she didn't have time to burn it, and leaving it in a trash can somewhere just meant Martin had a trail to follow. Maggie kicked them away and dressed in the thrift-store clothes. She even changed shoes. Anything to never have to wear canvas shoes again, and she'd be happy.

The one item she didn't hide away in the small bathroom in the RV was her book. She ran to Moundsville in such a rush, she completely forgot *The Source* was still tucked in the waist of her pants. She climbed into the front and set the book down on the console between the driver and passenger seat. Her phone landed in her cup holder and she started the engine with a wish and a prayer.

It took three tries, but the engine turned over and she pulled out of the storage unit. For ten seconds, she debated leaving the door open, but the minute it would take her to close and lock it could slow Martin down long enough for her to get safely out of Moundsville. The entire time she was out of the RV, she kept her eyes, ears, and nose open for any Gaze members who might be tracking her. She only climbed in behind the steering wheel once she was convinced no one was watching her movements.

Before she thought better of it, Maggie shifted the RV into gear and pulled out into the street leading to the highway that would take her to War. Without thinking twice, she grabbed her phone and pulled up directions. Just over five hours. It would be dark by the time she pulled into town.

Now was not the time to worry about when and where to stop. The RV had a full tank of gas and she had a lot of miles to put between her and the Gaze before she considered stopping for any reason other than filling up her gas tank.

Less than two hours and just under a hundred miles later, Maggie pulled off at the southbound rest stop on 77. So much for waiting until she got closer to War before stopping. But she needed the bathroom and could stand to grab a few bottles of water from the vending machine.

She washed her hands four times with the automated faucet in the rest stop's bathroom because her raccoon was not going to be satisfied with just one round. The air dryer, meant to conserve on paper towels, was as reliant as the stream of water. Which was to say Maggie had to contort her body just right to keep the constant stream of air coming.

She pulled the door open and almost crashed into the back of a man dressed in blue clothing. Either he was too wrapped up with his phone call or one of the true believers who sucked at his job but would do anything Zachery ordered because he didn't notice Maggie or her quick retreat into the bathroom.

Shit. Shit. Shit.

Crouching down, she looked through the vent at the bottom of the door.

"No. No one here's seen her..." The man paused as he listened to the voice through his phone. "I know her phone says she's here, Martin, but I swear, she's not."

Well, this was a bigger shit than before.

No wonder Martin hadn't chased after her. He didn't need to. All he had to do was look at some app on his phone and he'd find her no matter where she went.

Maggie fell on her bottom and scooched back against the wall covered in subway tiles. Probably easier to clean.

With a sharp shake of her head, she yanked her thoughts back to the problem at hand. How did she get to the RV while avoiding anyone else looking for her from the Gaze and what to do about the phone?

The bathroom had one window high up on the back wall, protected with a metal grate. Even if she got the grate open, she wasn't sure the window would open. The only way out of the bathroom was through the door and around the idiot Martin sent to grab her. The idiot might not recognize her scent through the bleach used to clean, but he'd smell her as soon as she walked by him.

"I'll just be a minute while I wash my hands. Don't touch anything and stop hitting your brother. No, just put your hands in your pockets and stand right there." The door opened and Maggie jumped to her feet as a woman, who looked as frazzled as Maggie's nerves, walked in.

The human woman's eyes narrowed on Maggie and her lips pursed, but she didn't say anything.

Most of the humans in Moundsville looked at the Gaze members with suspicion when they went into town, but the calculations going on behind the woman's eyes didn't seem to perceive Maggie as the threat.

"You better not be getting into any trouble out there!" The woman walked to the sink and washed her hands while watching Maggie in the mirror. When she finished washing, the woman stepped in front of the hand dryer closest to Maggie and waved her hands under the nozzle until the motor revved and hot air shot out. "I can get you a minute or two. Is that enough time?"

It took Maggie a few seconds to not only realize the woman was speaking to her, but also offering help.

Maggie nodded, not trusting herself to say anything.

"The creepy guy in blue, right?"

Again, Maggie nodded.

"Give me fifteen seconds, then head out. There's a custodian's office just out this door, with a door at the other end that leads outside. I saw it propped open when I came in." The woman shook her hands free of the last droplets of water and didn't wait for Maggie's answer before heading out the bathroom.

Then came the high-pitched scream of a woman.

Maggie didn't bother trying to decipher what the woman was carrying on about. Instead, Maggie counted back from fifteen. When she reached one, she pulled the door open. The area in front of the bathrooms was empty. Everyone in the rest stop had run to the woman who used words like pervert and creeper.

The office was right where the human said and Maggie walked in. Empty but for the cleaning supplies, an old desk along the back wall, and a filing cabinet. Maggie ignored everything, although her fingers itched to touch the knick knacks on top of the desk.

Once through the back door, she took a deep breath of freedom and then dashed to the RV. At least she had enough sense not to park right in front of the rest stop building. She hopped into the driver's seat, grabbed the cell phone, and scampered into the living part of the vehicle.

She could toss the phone, but the idiot Gaze member's sudden appearance spooked her enough to decide throwing it out wouldn't be enough. The phone had to die, and she didn't have many options. The battery slid free, and she flushed it down the toilet first. Next came the sim card with another flush. Finally, the phone went down the toilet with the last flush. She didn't bother filling the bowl with water before each flush, and she probably didn't even have to separate the parts of the phone, since it all landed in the same tank. But it eased her raccoon's anxiety and soothed some of her nerves.

As soon as the phone slid down the tubing, she got back behind the steering wheel and got the hell out of the rest stop. Frankly, it was a miracle she didn't back into anyone or thing, but maybe luck was on her side. The tires hit the freeway and Maggie breathed out a sigh of relief. She did her best to push aside the idea that her phone was the only way she could speak with her dad.

She wouldn't worry about that until she got to War and found a motel to check into. She wouldn't stay there, but it would buy her some time. If the Gaze knew she was headed to War, she could at least make them work to find her.

In retrospect, Maggie wouldn't know for sure whether it was a good or bad thing she pulled off at the rest stop. She leaned towards it being good overall, but there were a few minutes when she regretted letting something like a full bladder push her to making a stop before she was even two hours away from Moundsville and almost getting caught and dragged back to the compound.

CHAPTER TWO

DAMN it. What was taking the General so long? He was only a few steps behind them when Finley and Tevin headed down the trail that led to the garage. For being an old man and human, the General was surprisingly spry and held his own with the pack, but he wasn't moving fast enough for Finley's liking.

"I can't believe Vixen's making us wear this crap." Tevin tugged at the collar of the bullet proof duck jacket. "It's too hot."

Finley rolled his eyes. Sure, the body armor made things warmer than usual, but without knowing what they were walking into, Vixen hadn't been wrong with her order.

"And it's heavy too." Tevin slumped down in the front seat of the SUV.

Finley closed his eyes and counted to five. Slowly. It was a miracle Tevin was still alive. In the nine years Finley had been at Broken Peak, Tevin hadn't gotten any less annoying. If anything, he had gotten worse.

Especially since Foster, Jackson's four-year-old kid, arrived. Hell, Foster might even be less annoying than Tevin.

Tevin sighed. Loudly. Not for any other reason than to make sure Finley knew just how annoyed he was with the entire situation.

"Is the air on? Turn the air on."

"Damn it!" Finley slammed his palm down hard on the top of the steering wheel. "Get out. Just get out. The General and I can handle this on our own if it's such a fucking hardship."

Tevin gaped at him. "Sheesh, what crawled up your ass and died?"

Finley reached across the front seat and opened the door. "Just get out. You don't want to be here and we don't need any fuck-ups in town."

"I'm not going to fuck it up," Tevin protested.

Finley glared at him. Pack hierarchy was kind of odd. Tevin had been at Broken Peak longer than Finley, but Finley was older. It wasn't the weight of the body armor that Tevin was really complaining about. He was pissed that Finley was driving and the de facto leader of their impromptu mission. Finley didn't care much either way, but Tevin didn't like the reminder that not only was he the youngest (ignoring Foster) but also the lowest ranking member of the pack. Which wasn't saying much, since Broken Peak was overflowing with dominant shifters, each one capable of taking on the role of Alpha of their own pack at some point.

When Tevin still hadn't gotten out of the SUV, Finley turned so his back was to his door and was prepared to kick Tevin out. Literally.

"All right, all right. I'm going." Tevin slid out, stuck his hands in his pockets and strolled out of the massive garage as though nothing happened and leaving was all his idea.

Finley grabbed his phone and after going through the thumbprint, eyeball scanning thing, and voice recognition Danielle had set up to keep the pack's communication lines secure, he called Allard.

"Less than ten minutes. Didn't even make the over-under." Allard laughed from the other end of the line. "I'll be there in a few."

"How did you–never mind. I don't even want to know."

"Probably not. I'm on my way." Allard ended the call with the same formality as when he answered it.

Finley took the time waiting for both the General and Allard to recheck the gear, make sure the weapons were all loaded and stored properly, and his protective shirt and vest didn't have any defects.

All the things he should have been doing instead of listening to Tevin's hissy fit.

"Move the gear to the Range Rover." The General's voice held the same level of command as Vixen's and Bray's, but he didn't have an animal inside of him to help push the order.

And yet, Finley obeyed as if Vixen had issued the order herself. He didn't even ask why.

Allard stepped up to the back hatch, waiting for Finley to release the door. "Shit, Fin, did you bring half the arsenal?"

Finley shrugged, "I didn't know what to expect."

"Better safe than sorry, boy." General Jesup climbed into the back seat of the Range Rover while Allard and Finley finished transferring the gear.

"Does Vixen know I kicked Tevin out?"

The General snorted.

"He probably called and complained as soon as he was out of earshot."

"He did," General Jesup confirmed.

"Was she pissed?" Finley asked as he climbed in behind the steering wheel.

The General reached into the front seat and patted Finley's shoulder. "She trusts you and she trusts your judgment."

Allard slammed the back door closed and trotted around to the passenger side. He jumped in next to Finley and slapped the dash with his palm. "Danielle's on the line, she'll give us more info once we get closer to War."

Finley started the older model SUV that might as well have been a tank in a previous life and shifted it into gear. As he neared the massive doors of the garage, Allard pressed the button to open the doors. As soon as Finley had enough room to clear the doors, he drove through them and onto the old lumber road that came out on the country road that would take them into town.

"Foster's complaining that you didn't wait for him to shift back so he could go with you guys." Danielle's voice came from the car's speakers.

Allard must have paired his phone to the navigation system Danielle had installed in all the vehicles. The woman was a technical genius and updated everything from the Pack's security system to the cars and phones they used. When it came to computers, Danielle was a magician, and she was using her magic to help them find the shifter her computer program claimed was in danger.

"Tell him he can come with me next time." Finley smiled, even if Foster couldn't see it. The pup kept Finley on his toes with all his questions, but he loved the little guy. The others tolerated Foster because that's what packs did. Protect their pups. Jackson and Eleanor might be the kid's parents, but Finley was Foster's favorite uncle, and he wouldn't give up that role for anything.

"We'll tell him you promised to take him for a run. Eleanor is channeling a mama bear, and I don't think she's going to let Foster leave Pack territory until the kid's at least eighteen." Leighton was amused by Eleanor's over-protectiveness if the laughter in his voice was anything to go by. A muffled smacking sound followed Leighton's laughter. "Ow, woman, what was that for?"

"Because when we have kids—"

"We're having kids?"

"Well, yeah, you just asked me to be your mate, and I said yes. Kids are going to be part of that, aren't they?"

Finley rolled his eyes and muted the conversation.

"What if she has information for us?"

"She's too busy being all lovey-dovey with Leighton and no one should be forced to listen to that." Finely glanced in the rear-view mirror at the General to gauge his response, but he was looking out the window at the passing scenery. "I'll take her off mute when we get closer to town."

Allard raised an eyebrow, but said nothing.

"What?"

"Nothing."

"Your thoughts are practically shouting at me."

Allard snorted out a laugh hidden behind a cough. "You can't read thoughts any more than I can." Danielle had been convinced the shifters could read thoughts, and her belief was a running joke between the pack members. What shifters could do was read signals from body language, especially humans who weren't as adept at hiding their emotions.

"Well, you're shouting your thoughts at me right now."

"Okay then, what am I thinking?" Allard crossed his arms over his chest and leaned back in the seat.

"That I'm being as stupid as Tevin."

"No, I wasn't thinking that. I was wondering what Leighton said that made you decide you didn't want to hear anymore."

"It's always odd watching Vixen interact with you. She always cared about her teammates and the soldiers she rescued from critical situations. But the way she is with you is different. Sometimes I have difficulties reconciling my Vixen with your Vixen." The General offered his observation while he continued staring out the window.

Allard glanced over at Finley while eyeing the General in the back-seat from the corner of his eyes before turning away.

Finley drove on in silence for another two minutes. "Fine. I muted them because I'm tired of the coupling going on. It's like matchmaker central. Bray and Vixen were great. We needed an Alpha female, but then came Eleanor and Jackson and his ready-made family. Now it's Danielle and Leighton. Aren't we supposed to be preparing for leading our own packs? How can we do that if we're all pairing up?"

The last bit of Finley's rant was rhetorical, but Allard didn't care.

"Bray struggled with us when he didn't have a mate. It's a miracle he didn't kill Tevin at least a hundred times over. A bachelor Alpha can only lead a pack of bachelor Alphas for so long before they tear each other's throats out." Allard didn't look at Finley as he spoke. "Leighton's the most dominant of all of us, but without Danielle, he'd never be ready to lead a pack. Besides, what makes you so sure we're destined to lead our own packs?"

"Fine, whatever. You can have your prophecy thing with Mac and Eleanor. I'm just tired of the honeymoon crap going on."

"Is it really that bad?"

"Yes."

"In a paraphrasing of the immortal words of the bard, the man doth protest too much, methinks." The General winked at Finley in the rear-view mirror with a self-satisfied smirk.

Finley grumbled something unkind under his breath and unmuted the phone.

"–where the hell are you? We see the Range Rover moving, but you aren't answering. Do we need to send out a rescue mission?" Leighton's voice cut through the speaker. "Should I call Vixen?"

"No, we're in town. Where are we going?"

"There's an RV park, wedged between the Tug Fork and Rocket Boys Road. I'm sending the coordinates to your nav."

"That's a park? I thought it was a graveyard for RVs." Allard pressed the screen until it displayed directions to their destination.

"Yeah, well, you're not going to like that there's only one way in and out." Leighton's voice came through the speaker. "The coordinates Dani sent you lead to the unofficial back way in. The road dead ends and as near as we can tell doesn't have any association with the campground, but it's the safest way in and out."

Finley glared at the brake lights on the car in front of them. "Great."

"You'll thank me later." Leighton must have pushed Dani away from the microphone since his voice came through louder than before. "We'll stay connected, but we're gonna mute ourselves here. Let us know when you get there."

Allard glanced at the screen, "looks like we're less than ten minutes away."

The line went silent and no one in the car spoke. At least Finley wouldn't have to listen to whatever it was couples talked about. But five minutes later, he couldn't stand the silence.

"It's not that I don't think about finding my mate someday."

"Never thought you did."

"Never had you pegged as the one I'd have to bash over the head with a two by four." The General cleared his throat. "You're having the same problem I am. Reconciling those you knew with the changes that came when they met their mates."

"What? Yeah. I guess." Finley growled at the braking lights. "You ever think about what your mate might be like, Allard?"

"Not particularly, no. But then, not all of us are lucky enough to mate with our mates."

"What's that supposed to mean?" Finley pulled around the dark blue sedan and pressed his foot down on the accelerator to get around the slow-moving car before another car came barreling down the county highway in the opposite direction. "You're spending too much time with Mac if you're buying into that prophecy bull crap."

"Come on. Vixen shows up in our territory and she's not human *and* strong enough to deal with us. Don't you think there's something more going on?"

"No."

"Okay, fine, but what about the others? You can't ignore Eleanor researching Mac's ancestor before coming here. From what she said, she was interested in Appalachian magics before she adopted Foster."

Finley ignored Allard. He made more sense than Finley was willing to admit at that particular moment. Except Allard wasn't letting it go. Just as he opened his mouth, the nav screen pinged and flashed a red circle at the road where Finley was supposed to turn.

"Saved by the bell." Allard smirked at his friend.

"Yeah, right. You'll just find another opportunity to tell me whatever it was you wanted to lecture me about." Finley leaned forward over the steering wheel and peered out the front windshield. "Shit, where the hell is she sending us?"

The road wasn't a road. It wasn't paved and hadn't ever been from the looks of the tree branches hanging over the dual tire tracks that hadn't seen actual tires from a car in years, if not decades. He braked until the speedometer barely hit five miles per hour, so he could better avoid the detritus littering the ground.

"The better question is what's so bad to cause someone to stay in a place like that." Allard bent his head toward the campground that came into view as the Range Rover approached the edge of a culvert.

The campground might have been nice when it first opened, but Finley doubted it. Maybe fifteen RVs sat parked in groups of three or four and except for three, they had been parked there for years if the dead grass and weeds were an accurate measure.

"Which one do you think is hers?" Finley asked.

"Usual bet?"

"Sure." Finley grinned in response. Allard and Finley never bet with money or even objects. They wagered chores. Finley wasn't sure who did whose chores more often, but now that they were older, they wagered patrols. Nothing that would put the Pack at risk, just giving up a good patrol time for a less enjoyable one.

"Chevy van. It looks like it just arrived from the lack of dead grass poking its way into crevices." Allard offered the reason for his pick, but everyone in the Range Rover knew it wasn't the real reason. Sure, it played a role, but the real reason was it looked as though it was on its last wheels. Exactly what someone running might buy.

Finley might have picked that one too, if the Sunrader hadn't caught his attention. Clean, rust free, and it even had a rainbow racing stripe down the side. The perfect RV someone might have bought a few years ago and stored away with the idea of running. "That Nissan Sunrader."

"Really, it has to be forty years old, at least."

"And it probably still has orange upholstery and green shag too."

"Probably." Allard glanced over his shoulder to the backseat. "Wanna get in on this?"

"I'm fine." The General continued looking out the window, as if he expected a team of commandos to jump out from behind the trees at any moment.

"Which one is it, Dan-Dan?"

"Dan-Dan? You've been spending too much time with Foster, Finley." Danielle's disembodied voice responded. "To answer your question, I'm not sure. I can't get a read on the Chevy's license from the satellite. But if we're continuing with the raccoon theme Ms. Iotor is embracing, it's the Sunrader. The title and registration goes into a giant black hole that leads to no one, and from what I can tell, it hasn't been driven more than a few miles every year for eight years."

"You can take tonight's patrol."

"Hold on, we don't have confirmation yet."

Finley opened the car door and stepped down. "Lead the way."

"Guys. Hold up." Leighton interrupted their chatter. "Gazes aren't exactly normal. If she's running, which she definitely is, they'll want her back and do whatever they have to. They won't care if they have to hurt humans or other shifters. And she's gonna be skittish. I'd be surprised if she doesn't run if she spots you before you find her. Plus, she'll see you guys coming a mile away."

"Great. Any suggestions?"

"Sit back and watch. And if you see her, don't approach her. They might be smaller than wolves, but a raccoon shifter will have no qualms biting most of your face off. She'll leave just to see what you guys do and when she does, leave a note or something."

"Now you tell us." Allard shook his head at the news. "If I knew we'd be staking out a campground RVs go to die, I'd have brought snacks."

Finley got back in the car and closed the door. "How come I'm guessing you knew all this when you gave us these cords, Danielle?"

"Would it have changed anything?"

"Probably not."

"Muting the mic now. Will keep you updated with news as it arrives."

"Ms. Howe?" The General asked.

"Yes?"

"How many touches?"

Touches, as Finley and Allard learned before Vixen sent them on a mission that might end with their faces bitten off, referred to how many times others referenced a phone number, either in text messages, voice mails, or actual phone calls. Last they heard, the woman they were looking for had over four hundred touches.

Danielle didn't answer right away, which didn't bode well for one Maggie Iotor. "It's almost doubled."

"Can you triangulate?"

"Already trying to come up with something. It's just hard to do and not get caught. When I learn something, I'll let you know." The line went silent.

"So..."

"We wait." The General answered Finley's non-question. "And watch both RVs."

They waited, and they watched.

Finley sighed and Allard stretched.

The door to the Chevy van opened and an older man with a stomach creeping down over his belt stepped down to the ground and looked around the camp. From the sneer on his mouth and the wrinkles on his nose, he wasn't happy with the camp he was parked in. He scratched the back of his neck, turned, and returned to the RV's interior.

"Looks like you won. Bruce doesn't come across as a Margret and there's no indication he's looking for anyone."

"Bruce?"

"His stomach."

"So you named the man's stomach in the few minutes we saw him?"

"I named both the man and his stomach."

The General might have groaned. Or maybe it was his body making the noises.

Allard and Finley shared a look. Vixen made the same types of noises when she didn't want to use words. When Vixen used it, the sound usually meant get your heads back in the game.

They stopped their chatter and waited some more.

A little over an hour since they drove through the forest to the perch on the edge of the culvert, Leighton's voice came through the speakers. "Any sign of her?"

"Not yet." Allard pressed his fingertips against his closed eyes.

"Chances are she isn't there then. She'd be curious enough to pull you closer."

"Leighton, how the hell do you know so much about raccoons?"

"I lived right next to a Gaze. They aren't like other shifter communities. Imagine all the worst cults from the humans and mix them all together with a sprinkling of some serious what the fuckery and the business practices of a drug kingpin or Mob boss. That's a Gaze."

"Well, that doesn't sound good at all."

"The leader of the Gaze by me used the young women to bring in money. They were told to go out and bring money back by any means. Some bought into the Gaze enough that they did it all willingly. Sort of. Others required motivation."

Finley's wolf growled and Finley agreed with the sentiment.

"Shit." Allard spoke for everyone in the car.

"Can you tell if anyone else is watching?"

"Doesn't look like it."

"Okay. Leave a note for her. Vixen says to give her directions to Broken Peak."

Allard leaned back in the seat and crossed his arms over his chest. "You sure? We don't even know who this girl is."

"Yep." Danielle's voice didn't waver. "Unless she's planning on blowing up her Gaze, or whatever they call the hell where they live, she's the one in danger. And if she intended harm to her Gaze, Vixen would be leading the charge."

"Anything we're supposed to include in the directions?"

"Yeah, write them for her animal and not her. And make sure you hit the landmarks where we have cameras set up."

Finley pulled a pad of paper from the middle console and started writing with some help from Allard. Help Finley didn't need or want, but Finley's needs and wants had never stopped Allard before, so why turn over a new leaf now?

"I don't have an envelope." Finley folded the completed directions in half.

"Give it to me." The General reached between the seats and snatched the paper from Finley's fingertips.

When the paper came back to Finley, it was folded into a sort of envelope thingy. It reminded him of the little paper birds and flowers a kid in one of the foster homes he stayed at used to make. "Origami?"

"There's a lot of hurrying up and waiting in the military. Go on and leave the note for her so we can do our own hurrying up and waiting back at the Lodge."

"Hey, stop here for a minute." Allard patted Finley's arm. "There's the bookstore Jackson was talking about. Let me see if they have anything new."

Finley sighed but pulled into an open parking space on the street. "It's a used bookstore, how can it have something new?"

"You know what I mean." Allard was already out of the SUV and headed into the store. Eleanor loved old books and Jackson usually did something that pissed his mate off, so he learned early on to keep a stash of old books around.

"Would you look at that?" The General asked from the backseat.

"What?" Finley looked behind him, trying to see what General Jesup was looking at.

"That." The General nodded his head at the cheap motel across the street and halfway down the block. "The car with the three men standing around it looks awfully familiar."

Well, shit. The General was good at this shit. No wonder Vixen sent the older man with Finley and Allard. They would have fucked it up a few times over by now.

"I didn't think very many businesses in War had uniform requirements."

"What are they doing?"

"From the arm waving and half turns to look down the road, I'd say they are arguing about something. See the bigger guy in the back?"

"Yeah?"

"He's been checking his phone every few seconds. Like he's waiting for something."

Finley stared at the man the General pointed out. "For an order?"

"Probably. But what order would make three men stand outside a hotel instead of waiting inside their car or the hotel room?"

"A snatch and grab…" Danielle had used that phrase to explain the patterns her computer program used to identify Margret Iotor as someone to investigate. He got the gist of the phrase's meaning, but didn't fully grasp it until that moment while watching the three men loiter outside a hotel room. "Were they planning on pulling her inside their car and driving off?"

"Probably. Except she's not where they expected her to be."

"They don't know where she is…"

"Not yet, at least."

The idea of the three men grabbing Margret pissed off both Finley and his wolf. He hadn't seen the female, but his wolf sat up at attention when Finley approached her trailer when he dropped off the note and hadn't settled back down. His wolf pushed at Finley to do something. Anything. Even letting the animal out in the middle of town and the consequences be damned.

Finley jumped out of the Range Rover and jogged across the street, not paying any attention to the cars that slowed and honked at his audacity.

"And now we have a ball game." The General stood behind him, waiting for a break in traffic before following Finley into the motel parking lot. The old man might be spry, but he wouldn't win a match up with a car.

The males didn't so much as glance at Finley's approach. They should have recognized the wolf stalking them. That was their second mistake. The first was intending harm to the little raccoon shifter.

Stupid shifters.

Finley agreed with his wolf's observation.

He grabbed the closest male by the back of his collar and hauled him away from the others. Finley closed his left hand into a fist and brought it across his body and into the face of the idiot, just now noticing a wolf shifter was holding on to him. Bones snapped and crunched and blood spurted. The male grabbed his nose and bellowed. Finley dropped him and swung at the second male before he could sucker punch Finley.

Three against one should have had the advantage. They didn't.

Finley should have been working twice as hard to knock the others down while remaining on his feet. He wasn't.

The males lacked any genuine training. They didn't even have the strength Finley expected enforcers from any shifter group to have.

Each time one of the males pushed up to his feet, Finley met him with fists and feet. They'd be pissing blood for at least a week, even with the faster healing most shifters enjoyed.

"Stay the fuck away from her. She's under my protection now, and the next time I won't be as forgiving." Finley stepped down on the hand of the larger of the males, breaking his fingers.

"You could have waited for me to join in the fun." Allard headed into the middle of the brawl even though Finley had done a good job not letting the three males gang up on him.

The General reached out an arm and stopped Allard. "He has this."

Allard appraised the fight. The three males weren't giving up even though it was clear to anyone with half a brain cell they didn't stand a chance. He lifted his shoulder in what might have been considered agreement with the General's assessment. "What did they do to deserve the beating he's giving them?"

"Exist."

"Really?"

"Well, existing and loitering and not belonging and I believe intending harm to *her*, whoever her is."

"You don't say."

"That last bit came from Finley's mouth. I surmised the other parts."

"Considering our earlier conversation, I'd say the *her* part is a fairly interesting development." Allard was enjoying himself way too much if his commentary was anything to go by.

"Stay. The. Fuck. Away." Finley stood over the bleeding and groaning males. "And tell your boss or leader or whatever the hell you call the twisted fuck you follow, she's under the protection of Broken Peak now."

"She is?" Allard asked while trying unsuccessfully not to smile.

"Yes." Finley stepped over the broken males and crossed the street. "Are you two coming? Or do you want to release a press statement?"

"Oh, we're coming. Wild horses couldn't keep me away." Allard followed Finley at a much slower pace. He glanced at General Jesup as they crossed the street. "And what role did you play in that little drama? Which, by the way, you get to tell Vixen and Bray about."

"I merely pointed out to him that those three looked out of place."

"Sure you did."

The General chuckled and winked at Allard as they approached the running SUV with a grumbling and growling Finley sitting impatiently behind the steering wheel gunning the accelerator. "I dare say it will be interesting waiting for this Margret to arrive."

Both men stopped talking as they got into the Range Rover and remained silent until Finley turned off the main road on to the logging trail.

"I'm not a hundred percent certain, but I believe kicking the ever-loving shit out of three strangers might qualify as an over-reaction." Allard mused.

"Shut the fuck up." Finley's wolf growled in agreement.

"Perhaps we should turn back and stake out the campground for a little longer?" The General added from the backseat.

"With all due respect, General, you can shut the fuck up too."

CHAPTER THREE

MAGGIE sat on a low branch in a tree on the outskirts of the campground and stared at the RV she and her father had brought back from the dead over several years. The last place she expected to be was alone in an unfamiliar town. And the last thing she expected to be doing was waiting for a stranger to come back.

Her father should be with her. Not stuck at some compound with the one means of escape over five hours away parked in a rundown campground.

She'd watched the campground for a day and a half since coming back to find the folded up note stuck under the door of the camper. The sun was setting and unless she planned on sitting around watching for another day, Maggie had to make a decision. Follow the note's directions or ignore it, and the interesting scent of the wolf who dropped off the note left behind. He hadn't been careful about covering his tracks either. Like he wanted her to know he was there.

Her father had told her to find a shifter who wasn't a raccoon and lived in the area, maybe the shifter found her instead. She hopped down from the branch and headed toward her camper, sticking to the shadows as she moved across the quiet campground.

The directions hadn't included any major roads, just landmarks and other cues her animal would recognize. The note hadn't said to leave the camper behind, and she probably could have found her way to the territory if she wanted to bring the RV with. But she figured there was a good reason the directions didn't take her along Rocket Boys Road. Plus, she had a better chance of not being detected if she didn't drive up to their front door.

Maggie might not distrust the wolf who left the note, but she didn't trust him just yet either. She needed to watch and make sure she wasn't hopping into the frying pan from the fire. Of course, that meant leaving most of her things behind. She slipped into the camper and found the small canvas bag with a drawstring closure. A few years ago, she discovered her raccoon could wear the bag like a backpack. It was just big enough for a change of clothes, so she'd have something to wear when she wanted to walk on two legs instead of four. Plus, she could also bring her book and keys. Not that it would stop anyone from breaking in and hot-wiring the Sunrader, but taking the keys with her felt right.

A WOLF PUP BARRELED OUT the front door of the log cabin Maggie had been watching for the past week. She knew the pup well enough. He was a curious sort, always ready to play with the older and much bigger wolves, who were all patient and gentle with him.

She sat up on her hind legs and squinted her eyes.

Her raccoon's day vision wasn't as good as her night vision, so she couldn't see much during the day when the pack seemed the most active. Once she arrived in their territory, Maggie hadn't shifted back. She'd been in her animal body for so long, she worried that the animal would take over. The longer her kind remained an animal, the more difficult it was to push the animal back inside. It was a risk, but one she was willing to take.

Necessity couldn't always live in the same place as options and decisions.

She read that somewhere.

In a book.

She couldn't remember the title of the book, but that was okay. She didn't remember the title when she pushed the animal inside and allowed the female to emerge either. But she did know it was from a book. Her little beast hadn't completely taken over.

Yet.

She remembered it was from a book of proverbs.

Not *that* Book of Proverbs. No way in Hell Zachery would allow that particular book to contaminate the bookshelves of any member of the Gaze. No. The only books any member had been allowed to read had to be approved by Zachery.

She had followed the directions left for her, which was how she found herself in the middle of a remote area of the Appalachians and stuck inside her animal for the past week. Maggie needed to make sure the X at the end of the map didn't lead to some place worse than the one she came from.

So far she'd pieced together that bears, wolves, mountain lions, a coyote, a badger, and something she couldn't identify because whenever it came out, her raccoon took over, locked the woman side of her inside, and hid in the hole in her tree. Except for the not-human beastie, as far as Maggie knew, none of the kinds of shifters living in the region allied themselves to the Gazes.

Smart beasts.

Well, that was something you didn't see every day.

The pup was running right to her. And scurrying along over the brown grass in front of the pup was a tan little rodent thingy sold in human pet stores.

Maggie couldn't remember what they were called, but it didn't matter because the fat little roly poly was headed right for her.

Did it have no survival instincts whatsoever? Not that she made a meal of furry roly polys on the regular, but if they ran right into her paws? Well, who didn't appreciate a snack?

Maggie fought against her animal's instinct. Hard. Eating the roly poly wasn't smart in the scheme of things.

The roly poly wasn't stopping. Neither was the wolf pup.

Before instinct took over, Maggie pushed her animal aside and took over as much control as she could. It wasn't much, but it was enough. She darted the few feet out of the safety of the woods and grabbed the roly poly with her front paws and hugged it close to her chest while fighting all the instincts telling her to rub her paws around the roly poly.

Crapsicles.

She hadn't thought her plan through. Standing up on her back legs, she was barely the same height as the pup. The same pup who wanted what she had in her paws. The same pup who wasn't happy that he lost his prize. The same pup who latched on to the nape of her neck and was now trotting back to the house.

And the shifter standing on the porch that she just now saw as they closed the distance between the safety of the woods and the unknown of the house.

She twisted around in the pup's grip. At least he wasn't hurting her, but without releasing the roly poly, she couldn't get away.

Assuming the cabin in front of her didn't lead back to the Gaze, the roly poly was her ticket inside. She couldn't just drop it.

"Well, that's not something you see every day." The low rumbling, almost growly voice of the male caused her animal to push forward. Well, the sound of his voice *and* his scent. She'd recognize it anywhere after he left it all over her camper.

Her animal wanted, no, *needed* to see the male who spoke too.

Both animal and woman stared at the male standing at the top of a short set of stairs. Dark hair, long enough to brush the collar of his thermal shirt. Maggie's animal couldn't see what color his shirt was, but she thought it was blue or green.

Stupid animal. Maggie wanted to see him, but her animal wasn't giving up her body anytime soon.

"What did you find, Foster? A new friend?" The male asked with a soft chuckle.

Maggie's entire body shook as the wolf pup wiggled. She only just held on to the roly poly.

The male walked down the stairs with slow, careful steps and crouched down in front of all three animals. "You know better than to chase Hampstead."

The roly poly had a name. Good thing she hadn't eaten it.

The male held his hand out, palm up. "Why don't you give me Hampstead, then I'll make Foster let you go and no one risks getting squished."

Was he implying she would squish the roly poly? She hadn't taken a bite out of it yet. Besides, flattening things wasn't her style. Silly male. Maggie hissed.

Crapsicles.

Hissing was bad. Hissing always led to corrections from the enforcers in the Gaze.

She closed her eyes tight and shrunk back as much as possible while hanging from the mouth of a wolf pup.

A correction never came.

Instead, a warm laugh sent a fresh wave of tingles through her body.

Good tingles. Not the bad tingles warning her something painful was about to happen.

Maggie opened one eye.

The super sexy male was still crouched in front of her with his hand out, but he wasn't frowning or glowering. He full-on smiled at her, showing all of his perfectly straight teeth.

Maggie thought he had the nicest smile she'd ever seen. His smile was genuine, not the leering smiles of the males who worked closely with Zachery. Their smiles never reached their eyes. The smile she saw now not only reached the male's eyes, but caused funny crinkles at the corners.

"You're a spunky little thing, aren't you?"

Maggie opened her other eye and stretched her front legs out as far as they went, but she still didn't let go of the roly poly. That was her animal's doing.

Treasures were treasures, even furry ones.

The male reached behind his back. Maggie shut her eyes and pulled the roly poly back to her chest.

She had been wrong. A correction was coming.

"Hey, cutie, I have something for you. A trade."

His words didn't make sense. No one at the Gaze called her cutie or cute. They called her willful and prideful and sometimes stupid. And no one had ever offered her a trade. They just took.

She opened both eyes. The male's hand was still reaching out with the palm up, but his other hand held something shiny. Something that no one in the Gaze would ever allow her to hold on to for very long.

A pocket knife! And not one of those dinky ones either. The one he held out to her was as big as his palm.

Neither her animal nor Maggie had to think about it for long. She reached her front legs out and dropped the roly poly in the open palm, then snatched the shiny before the male could take it away.

Ha. She had a shiny!

And not just any shiny, it was a sharp shiny.

She had a *sharpy*!

She chittered happily while running her paws over the object. It was still warm. Like it had been close to the male's body. And it smelled like him. The raccoon wanted to run her nose all over it, but Maggie thought sniffing a knife might come across as weird and convinced her animal she could smell away once they were in private. The excitement over the sharpy was enough to distract her from the fact she was still hanging from the mouth of the wolf pup.

"You like it?"

Like it? She loved it. Maggie might have even been singing a silly song about her sharp shiny. She chittered back at him and hoped the male understood.

"If Foster lets you go, will you stick around?"

Whoa there. The chittering halted.

"Don't run away, okay?" The male's smile was still there. "You're safe here. I promise."

Maggie believed him. She could tell if he lied, but she didn't need that sense to know she could trust him.

She chittered. Or maybe her raccoon chittered. At this point her animal had enough control that Maggie pushing her to run away might well be impossible.

The male's smile grew even bigger. "Okay, Foster, let her go."

The wolf pup whined, but didn't let her go.

Crapsicles. Of all the possible ways this scenario could have played out, the wolf pup not letting her go hadn't crossed her mind.

"Foster, don't make me get Vivi." The male stood with an effortless grace and covered the roly poly with his free hand before the furry thing could make another escape.

Maggie didn't understand who Vivi was or why she, or it, was a threat, but Foster dropped Maggie. Which under most circumstances would have been good. Except, no way in hell was her raccoon releasing the sharpy. Maggie tottered on her hind legs and side-eyed the three steps. It wouldn't be the first time she climbed steps on her hind legs, but it hadn't been pretty those other times and it wouldn't be now.

Her raccoon had enough sense to hold on to the sharpy with one paw and keep the other paw free so when she fell, which was a strong possibility, her snout wasn't at risk of being flattened.

What an embarrassing grand entrance.

CHAPTER FOUR

SHE waddled up the steps, thankful the male wasn't behind her and for her free paw that found the railing. Although, her front legs weren't as long in proportion to her back legs and the three steps felt like Mt. Everest.

Foster hopped around her with his tail wagging.

Not helpful. When she hissed at the rambunctious pup, it wasn't her animal making the noise. It was all Maggie. The raccoon was too busy keeping balance to worry about the wild antics of an over-excited juvenile. But then her animal wasn't fond of the younger kits in the Gaze either and ignored them most of the time.

As soon as she made it up the final riser and was certain she wouldn't fall backwards or sideways, Maggie grabbed hold of the sharpy with both paws. Walking, well waddling, on her hind legs might not be the best option, but that was on her animal.

"If I open the door, will you come in? I think Vixen might have some Oreos?" The male crouched in front of her so he looked *at* her animal instead of down.

Both Maggie and her animal liked it. But then her animal also liked Oreos, so the wave of happiness rolling through her body at that moment could have been caused by the offer of treats as much as by the male doing his best to keep her from having to tilt her head back and falling over.

After he gave Maggie the sharpy, there was nothing the male could do to upset her animal. Maggie opened her jaw and released a short chitter.

"Is that a yes?"

Maggie chittered again.

"I'm taking that as a yes." The male stood, and when he got to the front door, he secured one hand around the furry thing and used his now free hand to open the door. He held the door open for both Maggie, who continued her awkward waddle on her hind legs because of the sharpy, and the wolf pup, who alternated between hopping around the male in an attempt to get the roly poly and bouncing around Maggie because she supposed her animal was like a shiny to him.

"I'm Finley and you already met Foster and Hampstead."

Finley.

That was a pleasant name to go along with his delightful smell.

Wait. Where did that thought come from?

Silly raccoon thinking nice names and smells were a good thing.

And Oreos. Apparently her raccoon was a sucker for the mere mention of an Oreo.

"There are going to be a lot more shifters where we're going, but don't worry. I promise, no one will hurt you." The nice male continued carrying on a one-sided conversation as though she was answering him.

Not that her raccoon had stopped chittering since she waddled her furry butt inside. But Maggie couldn't say for sure what her animal was going on about, except images of Oreos and pocket knives flooded her thoughts.

"Well, this is something you don't see every day." A powerful female, the one who wasn't human, stood up from a large table in the middle of the kitchen and stared down at Maggie.

Her animal wanted to run back to her hidey hole in the tree, but Maggie stopped her animal's instinct for flight, remembering what Finley with the friendly voice and smell promised.

No one would hurt her.

Finley handed the roly poly over to a human female in the room. "Foster chased Hampstead outside and came back with her."

"Oh my God, look at her hands!" The woman holding the roly poly screeched.

Maggie wanted to cover her ears, but that meant dropping the pocketknife. Something her animal was not on board with. All the other males, and there were a lot in the room, either lifted their shoulders or covered their ears. Maggie bet none of their animals coveted shiny things so much they'd be willing to suffer through the discomfort of high decibel noises.

"Dani, babe, I know you're excited, but maybe not so high with your voice, yeah?" One of the males wrapped his arm loosely around the woman he called Dani's neck and pressed his lips against her temple. "Why don't we put Hampstead away?"

The male led the squealing woman out of the kitchen and down a hallway.

Another male scooped up the pup and followed the couple. "Come on, kid. We'll get you all shifted back and then you can properly introduce yourself to your new friend."

The not-human female stared at the others in the kitchen, and Maggie maneuvered her body behind Finley's legs.

"Yeah, no way I'm leaving, Vixen." Another human female sitting at the table spoke while grinning at Maggie. "Jackson took care of Foster, and Leighton and Danielle have the hamster handled. I'm not missing this one."

Vixen. That's what they called the not-human woman. Maggie filed away the other names for when she shifted back and tucked her animal inside.

"I sort of promised her Oreos."

Maggie clamped her mouth closed before her raccoon's chittering hit a pitch close to the squealing woman, Danielle.

"Oh yeah, I'm sticking around for this." The human woman jumped up from the table and ran across the kitchen to a door in the back of the room. "Double stuff or regular?"

Was she asking Maggie? Her animal assumed the question was directed at her and added chattering to her chittering.

Boooooth.

They won't understand you, silly beast.

Don't care. Boooooth.

Finley looked down at Maggie and smiled at her animal. Her raccoon couldn't have cared less, but Maggie enjoyed his attention. She smiled back up at him and hoped the facial expression didn't turn her face into a grotesque caricature of a crazy animal.

"How about I help you to the table and you can meet the others while Eleanor finds some Oreos for you?"

He didn't need to ask twice. Her animal climbed him like, well, like a tree. And she didn't drop the pocketknife once. It didn't even slip. Finley cradled her body in the crook of his elbow and carried her to the table. Instead of putting her down on a chair, he sat down and shifted her from his elbow to his lap. Her raccoon should have protested the indignity of sitting in someone's lap, but instead she reveled in it.

Seriously? There's no coming back from this.

Oreos.

Maggie considered pushing her raccoon back inside her, except sitting on Finley's lap without a stitch of clothing on was even more undignified. Once she was back in control, she and her little beastie were going to have a long conversation about acceptable behavior.

"Danielle's going to kill me for not taking a video of this." Eleanor placed several packages of cookies on the table.

"You are not taking videos of her like she's some viral thing on social media." Finley growled low and his chest shook with the noise.

Instead of bolting, like she expected her raccoon to do, she rubbed her back against his chest and returned his noise with a small grumble of her own. Yep. Maggie was having that conversation with her raccoon, and she'd make sure her goof of an animal had a better understanding of dignified versus undignified.

"I wouldn't do that. Please, give me a little more credit than that, Finley." Eleanor sat down at the table and pulled one of the cookie packages towards her to open. "But you have to admit watching her hands with that pocket knife, which is as big as her arm, is cute as hell."

Maggie pushed her raccoon aside and bent her head forward and down to see what her paws were busy doing. Unfortunately, raccoon shifters took after their animal counterparts and oftentimes discovered their hands or paws doing the same movement over and over. That was the one good thing about Gazes. No one cared when you fiddled with a coin during an entire conversation.

"It's practically obscene." One of the males snickered.

The male wasn't wrong. Her raccoon held the pocketknife in one paw and stroked its length with the other.

The way her raccoon sat happily on the undignified side of the scale and didn't look to be making any plans in the near future to move closer to dignified, it would have been so much better to just fall flat on her face when she waddled up those stairs.

"There she is." Vixen slid into the chair across from Maggie and peered at her raccoon. Vixen pulled an Oreo from the package and held it out to Maggie. "Don't mind Tevin, he can be a bit of a prat sometimes."

As soon as the cookie came into view, her raccoon took back over. Except there was a problem. Her raccoon wasn't letting go of the knife, but she needed both paws to hold on to the cookie and satisfy the animal's fixed action behavior. Maggie just knew it was going to be bad.

Her raccoon considered the situation for all of ten seconds before sliding the knife into her mouth and holding it between her cheek and teeth, then leaning forward to snatch the cookie.

Yep, bad.

"That's not practically anymore. That is completely obscene."

Maggie closed her eyes and shrunk a little deeper inside her animal. There was no coming back from this one. At least her raccoon couldn't do anything more humiliating.

Her animal leaned back against Finley's chest and pushed the entire cookie into her mouth, along with the knife.

"I know you can hear me." Vixen, the not-human, spoke and Maggie used her raccoon's obsession with Oreos to push closer to the surface. "Once your raccoon has had her fill of cookies, maybe you'd like to make an appearance and take a shower?"

A shower would be amazing. As much as her raccoon enjoyed the water and didn't fight Maggie when she urged her raccoon to bathe in the river, it was too cold for Maggie to do more than take a sponge bath with the river water when she shifted back. If Maggie could have nodded without fear of everything falling out of her mouth, she would have. Instead, she settled for releasing a purring noise. The noise could have also been because Finley's thumb was drawing small circles along her side.

"Tevin, get her bag."

Wait. What? *Her* bag? They knew where her bag was? If Maggie could have narrowed her eyes at the not-human Vixen, she would have. They knew she was there the entire time?

Of course they did.

She was an unknown shifter in their territory. They probably knew the moment she crossed into pack land.

Sneaky wolves. Letting Maggie and her raccoon believe she was watching them without being seen.

"I'll get it." Finley wasn't asking permission from anyone. He spoke with such firm conviction, Maggie wondered if it wasn't more of a command than a statement.

"Dani's program picked something up, and she needed to check on it." Leighton, the male who left with the squealing woman, returned to the kitchen. "I brought you some of my mate's clothes. Just in case."

Maggie pushed her raccoon aside to get a better look at the male.

"I thought you'd be more comfortable." The male spoke with a soft voice and to her. "Finley will put you down and the rest of us will turn our backs, okay?"

Maggie almost wept. In almost twenty-five years, she had never experienced such kindness from anyone except her father. And even then, he had to be careful of his words and actions in case it got back to Zachery that her father was being soft.

"Finley, put her down." Leighton said.

Though Finley hesitated for a moment, he set her on the floor, then pulled out a chair and placed the clothes on the seat.

No one said anything, but they all turned their backs to her.

"This is the oddest thing I think I've ever done. And it kinda fits how weird this entire day has been." The male named Tevin said to no one and everyone.

While the others were distracted with a conversation about nothing, Maggie pushed her raccoon back and down. The stubborn beast pushed back, wanting more Oreos and not trusting that Maggie would take good care of the knife. Maggie promised and swore up and down that there would be plenty more Oreos and nothing bad would happen to the knife before her raccoon surrendered control.

She closed her eyes inside her animal and took a deep breath, and then Maggie was crouched on the floor and her raccoon was tucked safely inside. Unfortunately neither Maggie nor the Raccoon considered the physiological changes between animal and woman and the pocketknife was still in her mouth. Covered with wet Oreo crumbs.

She spit the knife out and wished for a glass of water or something to wash away the taste of chocolate covered iron from her mouth. But that could wait. First things first was getting clothes on, then figuring out what kind of weird pack she stepped into that welcomed an unknown shifter inside their home.

Oh God, everything hurt. She needed a long night's sleep in an actual bed instead of on a pile of leaves and fuzz. And a shower. In truth, Maggie could have found herself at Ed Gein's door and as long as a shower was on the table, she'd walk her ass right inside without a second thought.

She grabbed the clothes from the chair and pulled them on. The knife went into her pocket and then Maggie went to town adjusting the borrowed clothes so they fit her better. After a few minutes of attempting to roll the shirt sleeves and pants legs up enough so she could still walk without tripping and the conversation around her turning into random suggestions of what was the worst way to die, it was time to face the music.

"Did y'all think I was the Jolly Green Giant?"

"Oh my gosh, Finley, she's smaller than me, she'd fit in our pockets!" Eleanor clapped her hands excitedly.

A large presence hovered behind her, just next to her without touching. "She's not going into anyone's pocket."

Maggie turned her head and looked over her shoulder, then wished she hadn't.

Mine.

The image of the striking male standing behind her replaced all the images of Oreos and knives her raccoon had been pushing into her thoughts. She'd seen Finley through her raccoon and a few times from a distance when she needed to shift to stretch her legs. But apparently that wasn't close enough.

Finley's eyes weren't just blue, they were a glowing aquamarine. And her raccoon wasn't the only one who had thoughts that Finley was hers. Maggie was in a hundred percent agreement.

He smiled and Maggie almost went over. If his eyes didn't cause a full-blown case of swooning, then his smile ensured it. She didn't dare look anywhere other than his face for fear her raccoon would convince her to climb Finley like a tree again and she wouldn't do anything to stop it.

"Hi, I'm Finley."

"Maggie." Yeah, she managed to say her name, but even that took more concentration than she wanted to admit.

"Maggie?" Vixen asked.

Something about the not-human's voice compelled Maggie to turn away from Finley.

"I'm Vixen, that's Eleanor. You know Finley, and the others are my mate, Bray, Allard, Tevin, and Leighton brought you the clothes. I'm going to tell you the same thing said to me and what I've said to the others. As long as you are here, no harm will come to you."

CHAPTER FIVE

"IS THERE a reason you're tagging along?" Finley shoved his hands deep in his pockets and trudged across the lawn into the woods.

"Not particularly. Mostly because I figure it will be more entertaining to watch you than it would be watching Tevin and Bray fight about something random." Allard caught up with Finley and bumped against his shoulder.

"And why am I so entertaining?" Finley stood just inside the woods and relied on his wolf's heightened sense of smell to point him in the right direction towards Maggie's tree. He liked the name Maggie. Margret was so old-fashioned, and it didn't fit either the raccoon or the tiny female as well as Maggie did.

And shit, she was tiny. Eleanor hadn't been kidding when she said Maggie could fit in their pockets. He didn't think she stood much more than five feet tall, if that. Although her mass of wild brown curly hair might have added a few inches to her height. No way she could have handled the three males sent to grab her. Hell, three was overkill. Just sending the bigger one would have been enough.

His wolf growled at the thought of Maggie being taken against her will by anyone. Big or small. Finley agreed with the sentiment.

"Because your wolf is growling and you're scowling, and I'm willing to bet a week's worth of chores, that thoughts of the delightful Maggie have something to do with both."

Finley's wolf snarled at the word delightful. No one needed to be calling Maggie delightful, especially not Allard, an unmated wolf.

Shit.

Where had that come from?

Allard laughed and bumped into Finley's shoulder again. "Considering how you've been acting since we found her camper in War, think maybe Maggie might be more than just a phone number pulled out of thin air by Danielle's program?"

"Nope. It's just my wolf being protective. Sort of like with Foster."

"Fin, you've never growled at anyone about Foster." Allard grinned, but at least he wasn't laughing this time. "Admit it, this is different. You didn't even want Tevin going out to get her bag."

Finley stopped in the middle of the trail and used his wolf's sense of smell again to find Maggie's tree. "That's because Tevin's an ass and probably would have written his name on all her things."

"He's an ass, yes, but he hasn't written his name on anything in a while."

"He wrote his name on the soap. On the fucking soap."

"That was two months ago."

"Two months isn't a while."

"So, you're just going to ignore beating the crap out of those raccoon shifters in War and your wolf's growling and snarling."

"Yes." Allard had a point, but Finley didn't care much. "Besides, it's not like Broken Peak is safe right now. Even if the attacks are coming less frequently, there's always the chance we'll have another helicopter crash into the side of the mountain."

"It's safe enough for Foster, Danielle, and Eleanor." Allard just had an answer for everything, didn't he.

"That's different." Finley stood at the trunk of a massive tree and peered up into its branches. Maggie's scent was strongest around the roots. They had a general idea where she hid and what she had with her because of the cameras, but Vixen had ordered them all to keep their distance until Maggie came to them, so he wasn't sure.

Finley eyed the branches and the trunk. There was no easy way up the tree for a grown-ass male. He should have brought Foster. That kid was part squirrel with how quick he scampered up trees. Of course, getting down was another story entirely. Reaching his arms up over his head, Finley jumped and grabbed the lowest branch, barely, then pulled his body up until he straddled the branch. Though most of the leaves had turned and fallen, he still couldn't see a hole, so he felt around the trunk until his fingers found his goal. The opening sat just behind another large branch, blocking anyone spotting it from the ground.

Smart little raccoon.

He reached inside and felt around for the bag. As soon as his fingers found the heavy canvas, he grabbed it and pulled it free. Finley jumped back to the ground.

Finley wanted to open the bag and peek inside. He wanted to discover more about Maggie, but it was light. Lighter than any of the bags the other males in the pack arrived with. It probably held a change of clothes and maybe a few other small things she called her own. When all you had to your name was a handful of things most others would consider trash and throw away, you didn't want to share them with anyone else. So looking at Maggie's things without her permission felt ten different ways of wrong.

"Why?" Allard leaned against the tree next to Maggie's and crossed his arms over his chest.

"Why what?"

"Why are Foster, Eleanor, and Danielle different?"

"Because there's gotta be a better place than here for her. Broken Peak shouldn't be her last chance like it was for the rest of us."

"Yeah, that's a stupid reason."

"Fine. I'm not ready for a mate, okay?"

Allard opened his mouth, but no words came out. He closed it, then tried again. This time he made some noises, but nothing that Finley recognized as an actual word.

"Vixen could hold her own against us. Hell, she even dropped Jackson. And Eleanor has some kind of magic with her voice that can convince us to do anything, even things we don't want, just by count-ing." Finley took pity on Allard and explained his reasoning.

"What about Danielle?"

"Leighton is like one step away from being a serial killer. I don't even like looking sideways at Danielle in case his wolf gets the wrong idea."

Allard shrugged and made a noise of agreement.

"When I take a mate, it's going to be because I'm Alpha of my own pack and can guarantee her safety."

"She'd be safe here, Finley."

"We don't know that. Bray and Vixen could change their minds and disband the pack. And then where would we be?" Finley slung the bag over his shoulder and headed back to the Lodge.

"They'd never do that."

"We don't know for sure. The same way we can't say with one hundred percent certainty the sun will rise tomorrow. We have faith that it will and haven't been disappointed yet, but I can't say the same for humans or shifters. If you put your faith in them, they're guaranteed to disappoint you."

"You need to put your faith in someone, Fin." Allard pressed his hand against Finley's shoulder blade for a moment, but dropped his arm to his side before Finley could push him off. "Sure, some might disappoint you, but what happens if they don't?"

Finley snarled low under his breath and continued along the trail at a faster pace. Maybe if he kept ignoring Allard, he'd finally get the hint and stop bothering Finley.

Yeah, right. Fat chance of that happening.

"Fin, wait up." Allard raced to catch up, but refused to keep quiet. "Okay, say you find a mate and she surprises you with how strong she is, what's stopping you then."

"Fine." He threw his arms up in the air in defeat. Allard just was not willing to let it go. "I want a mate and a family, but I'm not going to risk leaving them alone if something happens to me. I'm not willing to risk the chance of some government agency kidnapping my pups."

Allard snorted, but thankfully didn't say a word.

Not that confessing everything to his friend was what he intended, but if Finley had known it would shut Allard up, he would have said all that sooner. It would have saved him from a long walk through the woods made even longer because of the Chatty Cathy at his side.

Except Finley wasn't saved.

"Assuming you have pups."

"What's that supposed to mean?"

"Nothing." Allard shoved his hands in his pockets. "Nothing at all."

This time he kept quiet, and they walked back to the Lodge in relative silence. The only noises accompanying them came from the birds and other wildlife returning to their daily life behind the wolf shifters as they moved through the forest.

CHAPTER SIX

HOT water poured down from the shower, and Maggie stood directly under it. She never considered hot water a luxury before, but after days living in the woods, mostly in raccoon form, she swore she'd never take it for granted again. Of course many people said that all the time and a few days later they were forgetting to appreciate what they promised they wouldn't.

Maggie picked up the fresh bar of soap Vixen handed her when she pushed Maggie into the bathroom and told her to take her time. The heather scented soap was nothing like the bars of lye they made and used at the compound. It was more like the soap they made to sell at ridiculous prices.

Humans liked good smelling things. And if you slapped the words all-natural, handmade, and organic on something, the humans would pay ten times the amount it cost to make it.

She couldn't for sure say Zachery was defrauding the humans who purchased the crap they sold in the gift shop, but she had lugged a huge bucket of scented oil from the storage shed to the building where they made the soap and the fragrance had nothing natural in its list of ingredients.

While she lathered up the soap and began the simultaneously arduous and soothing task of wiping away the layers of dust and dirt and debris from her skin, Maggie categorized all the thoughts rambling through her mind into two categories.

What did she know? And what did she think?

She knew some members of the Gaze had been sent to find her and bring her back to the fold (she hoped it was a bring back alive mission and not a bring back dead or alive mission). She thought she had set a decent false trail in the town of War, and they didn't know for sure where she was.

She knew she was currently in the outskirts of War, far off the main roadway, and she thought she was safe.

She knew appearances could be deceiving, but she thought the shifters here were everything they seemed to be.

She knew Finley was sexy as hell, and apparently her raccoon thought he was hers.

Whoa there. What the hell kind of thought was that, and why was it running freely through her mind? Oh, this was not good. Not good at all. Maggie had no business thinking about any male except her father and how she could get him away from Zachery and the Gaze.

Maybe she needed to add no naughty thoughts about the male to the list of dignified and not dignified behaviors she wanted to drill into her easily distracted animal's head?

Apparently her animal was hanging around because the raccoon delivered the equivalent of a mental raspberry in Maggie's mind.

Oh, why didn't the pest go to sleep? She had days of practically being free, in the woods no less. She should be exhausted.

No.

Stubborn git.

Minnne.

No. No. Most definitely no. No distractions, and Finley definitely fell into the distraction category. Maggie bombarded her raccoon's mind with thoughts and images of the not-human Vixen. It had only been the promise of Oreos that kept her animal from running away when she found Vixen sitting at the kitchen table with the others.

Her raccoon pouted and sulked off, leaving Maggie alone once again with her thoughts. She would have placed money on the beast leaving Maggie alone so her raccoon could plot out her revenge.

With the soap in hand, the water still hot, and her raccoon plotting her revenge, Maggie returned to cataloging what she knew from what she thought. By the time the water lost its warmth and she grabbed a towel to dry off with, her thoughts were no longer a jumbled mess. The soft cotton of the fluffy towel absorbed the water without scratching her skin, and she added one more item to her list.

She knew the pack shared its wealth with everyone from towels to soap to food. It shouldn't count for as much as it did, but after a lifetime of sneaking little luxuries with her dad because Zachery reserved the best for his favorites, the fluffy towels and Oreos shifted to the top of the list.

Wiping clean the steam covered mirror, Maggie sighed at the image staring back at her. She did her best to untangle her mop of hair, but the lack of a brush made it an arduous task. Why hadn't she remembered to bring her brush with her from the camper? Oh right, her raccoon would have had to carry it.

Now or never, right?

Maggie breathed in deep then released the long breath. She checked the towel was secure around her chest and readied herself to face the non-human waiting on the other side of the door. Her instincts screamed at her to put the borrowed clothes back on, but she just couldn't bring herself to, not after they'd been next to her skin before she scalded all the dirt and grime from her body.

So, with only the towel as armor and a wild mop of hair for a helmet, she prepared for a potential battle.

Wait. The knife. She still had the knife Finley gave her. Maggie dug the knife from the pocket she slipped it into and wrapped her fingers around it. The cool metal pressed securely against her palm, even if it still had remnants of Oreos stuck to it, eased the lingering nerves. They were still there. She didn't think anything would erase all the nerves, but the knife settled them. She conveniently ignored who gave her the knife, but her raccoon hadn't.

Sharpy.

Maggie ignored her raccoon. She was done stalling.

Three females standing in the center of the room greeted Maggie as she stepped out of the bathroom. Two of them grinned at her with the smiles of crazy people. The human women. If Maggie had seen them in town, she would have crossed the street and kept going until she was one town over and sure she wasn't being followed.

The third female, the not-human, looked as if she was at her wit's end. Vixen had the same expression on her face as her father when Maggie came home covered from head to toe in mud. She looked behind, worried she'd done something to cause Vixen's expression of exasperation with the half-closed eyes and lips drawn together, keeping the words at bay.

The goofy grinning duo bounced on their toes and spoke at the same time.

Something about clothes and ordering more and making do with what they had. All sprinkled liberally with apologies. It didn't matter what they said or whether Maggie heard it, as long as they got their words out.

And that was the source of Vixen's exasperation.

"They aren't going to leave you alone. I'm apologizing now on their behalf." Vixen settled into one of the chairs in front of the bay of windows that looked out across the side yard. "You wouldn't know it from how they're acting right now, but both women are quite capable."

Maggie found herself smiling, even though she swore she wouldn't show any emotions until she was sure of her current environment.

"We don't think we have anything that will fit you. I have a pair of capris. It's a little cool outside for them, but you won't have to worry about the hems unrolling and tripping over them."

After spending so much time in the shower with her thoughts, Maggie kicked her mind back in gear and assigned a name to the woman with the purple hair who was talking.

"I like your hair." Maggie lifted her hand and combed her finger through her brown-colored hair, no different from anyone else's.

"Really?" Danielle clapped her hands together and squealed, much softer and not nearly as high-pitched as she'd screeched earlier in the kitchen. "If you want, we can color yours too. I need to order more and we can pick something out for you."

"And we can order clothes too. Not just hair color, if you want, that is." Eleanor, the dark-haired woman who looked as though she stepped out of a children's fairytale book, stepped in front of the bouncing Danielle and held out a bundle of clothes. "But until then, you can wear these. Or you can wear the towel if you want."

"Are you two kidding me? You all are worse than the boys in this pack, sometimes." Vixen pressed her palm against her forehead and right eye while shaking her head. "Maggie, trust me, they normally aren't like this, and while I'd like to say there's a good reason for their behavior, I'm willing to bet it has everything to do with you being a raccoon shifter and they've decided having a raccoon shifter as part of their pack is their new goal."

"That's not the only reason," Danielle protested.

"But it *would* be really cool."

"Their pack?" Maggie reached for the clothes and stepped behind a chair to dress. She looked over at Vixen while pulling on the pair of pants under the towel. "I thought it was your pack. Well, yours and your mate's?"

"Why do you think that?"

What Maggie wanted to say was both Vixen and her mate practically oozed Alpha vibes, but self-preservation took precedence, so she didn't. "Aren't you the Alphas?"

"Yeah, but it's as much their pack as mine. In fact, all the boys were here before me, so it's more *their* pack than mine."

Maggie's fingers fumbled with the button. Zachery was the Gaze leader and considered the Gaze and all its members his. All Gaze leaders followed that belief and enforced it as rigidly as Zachery. At least the Gazes with any influence and power did.

"Is Foster yours?" She asked Vixen, shifting the conversation away from pack dynamics.

"Eleanor and Jackson's."

"Mine."

The three females spoke at once.

"But aren't you..." Maggie pulled the long-sleeved shirt over her head and dropped the towel at the same time.

Before she asked what to do with the towel, Danielle took it from her and tossed it in the general direction of a basket in the corner of the room. "You can say it, she's a human and me too. And there's another human who stays with us, but he hasn't committed to fully moving in. Yet."

"Yet." Vixen reaffirmed Danielle's words. "Sit down, Maggie. Like I said earlier, no harm will come to you, I promise."

"I know you can tell whether she's lying. Or I think you can, but I couldn't. And Vixen said the same thing to me when I was standing in your same place. And I'm still here." Eleanor's goofy grin slipped into the reassuring smile as she sat in one of the chairs, as if the gesture might comfort Maggie.

It did. Which was weird, considering Maggie didn't know Eleanor at all.

"Yeah, she never said that to me. But Leighton did." Danielle's goofy grin turned even goofier.

"You'll have to excuse, Dani, Leighton asked her to be his mate and bond with him about a week ago and she hasn't come down from the clouds since."

Before she fell over from the shock of information they unloaded on her, Maggie fell into the chair. Lowering her chin, she lifted her gaze toward Vixen. "And you're okay with that?"

"Okay? Okay with what exactly?" Vixen enunciated each word as she spoke slowly.

"With their mating, I suppose."

"Why wouldn't I be?" Vixen tilted to the side in confusion.

"In Gazes, the leader decides all matings. And never with a human."

"We're going to have to move more chairs in here or Bray is going to have to give up part of the Great room to us." Danielle plopped down in the remaining chair and then promptly returned to the topic. "Pretty sure Vixen and Bray gave Leighton a shove, but there's no assigning mates here."

"Don't shifters have to have a connection to form a bond? That's how Jackson explained it to me. That as much as he decided he wanted me, his wolf played a bigger role in recognizing me."

"Same." Danielle nodded along with Eleanor's words and raised her hand. "What about you, Vix?"

"Similar, but different."

Danielle waved her hand in the air, as if brushing away an insect or bug. "Don't mind Vixen. She might look mean and talk in cryptic sentences, but she's really a teddy bear."

Eleanor snorted out a laugh and covered her mouth with her hand to muffle the noise. "She is, but she says she has a reputation to maintain in front of the males, so she keeps her soft and gooey center hidden."

"Are you two quite finished?" Vixen sighed with an exaggerated rolling of her eyes. "You promised not to get in the way and so far, that's all you've done."

"Vixen, you know I love you, right? So, I'm just going to lay it out for you. You're intimidating as fuck, and the only thing that kept Eleanor from running away was Foster and not having anywhere else to go. If I hadn't known you, I'd have wondered if the General was taking me to be retired. If we weren't here, Maggie would be half way across the country by now, looking over her shoulder to see if you were hunting her. Plus your animal..."

"She can be scary. She scares every single male in the pack except Bray, and I think that's only because the boys have driven Bray to secretly have a death wish." Eleanor added.

"I'm not that bad."

Both human women nodded their heads. "Yes, you are."

Vixen didn't correct the humans. She didn't yell or raise a hand. Instead, she shrugged, like she kind of agreed with what they said, even if it wasn't flattering. A flood of items joined the know list in Maggie's mind.

"Does Foster go to school here?" In need of processing all the new information she'd learned, Maggie asked what she thought was an innocent enough question.

"He's only four."

"Almost five." Vixen corrected Eleanor.

"Yes, almost five, as he's quick to remind everyone. For now we homeschool because, well, it's the only option available."

"The packs in the area don't have a school? I know there are other shifters here."

"Foster's the only pup, and while there are other shifters, Broken Peak is the only pack with mates." Vixen explained. "Did you have a shifter school?"

"No. We had a Gaze school."

"Really? How did it work? I've been relying on some others in the area to help with things I'm not great at. Like Danielle helps with math since I'm lucky if I can do addition without the help of my fingers."

"Um, well, I guess like most schools, we had classes in the morning and projects in the afternoon."

"Projects? Like plays or music or science experiments?" Eleanor asked.

"No... Some of us made soap. I didn't because I tended to spill things. A few helped construct buildings. Let's see, I think some girls worked in the gift shop. I know a few of the teenagers worked outside the compound."

"At human businesses?" Vixen's eyes narrowed, and though Maggie understood the pinched look from leaders to mean anger and correction, nothing about Vixen's posture gave Maggie any sign Vixen was angry at her.

"No. Zachery would never allow that. They helped sell things outside the compound."

"Who's Zachery, Maggie?" Despite Vixen's relaxed posture, her body thrummed with a tension powerful enough to urge the raccoon to emerge from her sulking.

"The leader of the Gaze."

Danielle and Eleanor shared a look, then looked at Vixen. Whatever they communicated back and forth with one another didn't require words, and Maggie couldn't decipher their expressions.

"I've left Foster too long alone with Jackson. I should probably check that they haven't destroyed anything."

"My computers will be feeling neglected. I need to go comfort them." Danielle hopped to her feet and hurried across the room, not even waiting for her friend.

"You know your computers aren't sentient, right?" Eleanor followed.

"Shh. Don't say that too loudly. Have you seen *2001: A Space Odyssey*? That's what happens when you say my computers aren't sentient."

The two women continued talking as they left the room.

"So..." Maggie smiled with the practiced smile she used whenever Zachery was close. "Humans? I don't think I've ever heard any stories about shifter groups accepting humans."

Vixen cocked her head to the side and drummed her fingers against the arms of the chair. "Aren't you curious?"

"About the humans? Yes, very much so."

"No, how we found you and why we invited you here."

Maggie looked out the windows and watched as two figures crossed the yard from the woods to the Lodge. As they drew closer, she recognized one of the males as Finley and her raccoon perked up. His long easy stride ate up the distance and as he neared the porch,

Maggie practically groaned. His lean muscles couldn't hide beneath the snug, long-sleeved shirt. With each step, the bottom of his shirt lifted, revealing the hint of the waistband of his underwear peeking above the tops of his low-riding jeans, which hugged his thighs and hips perfectly.

It should be illegal for that male to go out in public.

"Maggie?" Vixen snapped Maggie out of her day-dreaming.

"Yes?"

"Yes, you're curious?"

She lifted her shoulders with a slight shrug. "You don't seem all that bad."

"What did you have to lose then?"

"Yeah, I guess."

"But you didn't wonder at all how we found you?"

"My father said to come here. That there's a shifter here who isn't a raccoon."

"Ah," Vixen spoke as though Maggie's words explained everything.

Maggie mimicked Vixen's tilted head and blurted out words before she thought any better of it. "You don't make any sense." As soon as the words escaped, she covered her mouth. "I'm sorry."

"You don't have any reason to be sorry, Maggie." For a moment Vixen's eyes flashed a golden yellow. "This whole thing is confusing. For all of us, really, not just you. We have a way of finding information and we learned you were in danger. We want to help you, if we can, but we don't know why you're in danger."

Maggie stared at Vixen. To trust or not to trust.

Her raccoon stood firmly in the Vixen is scarier than even Zachery camp, but leaned to the scary being in a good way. From everything Maggie witnessed, no one else, not even the pup, was frightened of Vixen. The women had even teased her without any repercussions.

"I saw something I shouldn't have, and I ran away before Zachery found me. I left my dad behind because he couldn't come with me, even though we planned on leaving the Gaze together." Maggie blurted out.

"That's a lot to unpack." Vixen's voice softened to a near whisper. "So, let's start with the simplest. I'm assuming you're a witness to something Zachery can't have a witness to, so it's fair to say you aren't just in danger, your *life* is in danger."

Maggie swallowed hard and nodded.

"All right. From what Finley reported back about his visit to War and what you shared, it's not safe for you to leave Broken Peak. If you stay here, the pack can keep you safe."

"No shit!" A low rumbling growly male voice yelled from the other side of the door.

Maggie recognized Finley's voice right away.

Vixen ignored the interruption.

Maggie's raccoon didn't.

Minnnnnnee. The little monster added a tune to the word and began singing mine over and over. It was worse than the time Maggie hadn't been able to stop singing *The Lion Sleeps Tonight* for over a month since every time she forgot the damn song, someone walked by her singing the tune.

"We can't keep you here if you don't want to stay."

"The hell we can't!" Finley yelled once more through the door.

Vixen closed her eyes and inhaled. Maggie imagined she was counting.

"Excuse me for a minute." Vixen pushed up from the chair and stalked to the door. Nothing human remained in her gait, it was all animal.

Whatever the hell animal it was, she spooked the crap out of Maggie's raccoon, who returned to hiding in her sulking spot.

Vixen pulled the door open and Maggie leaned around the back of the chair for a chance at a glimpse of Finley. Even her raccoon stuck her nose up to catch some of his delectable woodsy scent.

"Yes?" Vixen asked.

Finley leaned from side to side to see over the top of Vixen's head. Once he spotted Maggie in the chair, his bobbing and weaving stopped and he smiled at her. Maggie smiled back and wiggled her fingers at him. Finley's smile widened, showing off his perfect teeth.

The better to eat you with.

Maggie willed her raccoon to shut up.

"What are you going to do about this?" The rumble of his voice sent tingles all through her body.

"Do you have any idea?"

"Yeah. She stays here. With me. With the Pack, I mean."

Maggie's cheeks heated with a blush and she ducked down in the chair.

"I'll take your suggestion into consideration. Did you find Maggie's belongings?"

"Yeah."

"Damn it, Finley, give me the bag and I'll make sure she gets it."

"She's not leaving."

"That's not for you to decide." Vixen shut the door closed with a thud as it banged into some part of his body. Probably his foot, thought Maggie.

"Like hell it's not." Finley yelled through the closed door.

"That boy..." Vixen grumbled as she turned away from the door and returned to her chair. She studied Maggie with slightly narrowed eyes, tilting her head from side to side. "Interesting..."

"Excuse me?"

"Oh, nothing." Vixen waved away Maggie's question with a swipe of her hand. "I want to remind you, again, no harm will come to you from anyone here. But before we go through your available options, one of which will be staying here as Finley suggested, I want you to meet someone. Are you okay with that?"

Maggie's head bounced up and down in quick agreement with Vixen. She wasn't sure what lay ahead, but staying at Broken Peak seemed to be the best option. And if the only payment was meeting someone, Maggie could manage.

CHAPTER SEVEN

"SO, these Gazes, how many are there? Do you know?"

Vixen had been asking general questions about the where's and how's of Gazes since she and her mate headed out the front door of the Lodge with Maggie.

From the time she was a kit, it had been drilled into Maggie not to speak about the Gaze with outsiders, and that habit reared its ugly head. Except the questions seemed innocent enough. Maggie didn't think she had shared any secrets. Not that she owed the Gaze anything, but she didn't want to put her dad in any more danger than he was already in.

"I don't know why you don't just invite him to join us instead of letting him slink around in the shadows." Bray glanced over his shoulder and gave Maggie a grin that was more grimace than smile.

"He's being punished."

"Vi, he doesn't know why he's being punished or that he's even being punished."

"If he asked, he could have joined us. I'm not going to make it easier on him by inviting him to walk with us instead of the fifty feet he's insisting on staying behind us."

Maggie grinned and stared down at her feet. At least she had shoes in her bag and didn't have to shove socks in the toes of a borrowed pair. Bray and Vixen continued their debate on whether not inviting Finley to join them actually qualified as a punishment since he wasn't aware of the punishment. The way they talked to one another was the way she imagined mated couples should talk with each other, but never observed with her parents. Not for the first time, she wondered if love was possible in a mating. As far as she ever saw, none of the mated couples in the Gaze actually loved one another. Zachery used matings to keep control of the gaze. Eventually bonds formed, and the breaking of a bond almost always resulted in death.

"Are you questioning my judgment, Bray?"

"Vi, you chose me, I'd never question your judgment." Bray wrapped his arm around Vixen's shoulder and pulled her against him.

"Maggie is our witness."

"Yep." Bray looked back at Maggie and winked while reaching for her.

He didn't actually touch her, but used his hand to encourage her to walk next to them instead of behind him. Maggie jogged forward and slipped in beside Bray. Bray's wolf didn't frighten Maggie's raccoon nearly as much as Vixen's animal.

"Vixen says your father is still living with your Gaze?"

"Yes, sir."

"Oh, hear that, Vi, she called me sir. How come none of the others call me sir?"

"Because they're lost boys, Bray, and you're their Peter Pan, not their Captain Hook. They aren't suitably scared of you." Vixen bumped her hip against Bray's.

Maggie turned her face away from their intimacy. Right then, at that exact moment, Maggie decided she wouldn't mate unless she found someone who treated her like Bray treated Vixen.

"What happened to your mother?" Vixen asked.

"She's still there. It's why my father stayed instead of coming with me."

Vixen and Bray shared a look. A look she'd come to recognize as a reminder to just how fucked up her life with the Gaze was compared to other shifters. Maggie sighed.

"I don't think your definition of a mating is similar to mine. They're mated and there's a bond. The bond took a while to form. But it's there. If my dad left before it had weakened enough, the separation would kill him."

"You never considered leaving with your mom?"

Maggie pushed down the memory of the last time she was alone with her mother. She'd practically pushed Maggie at Zachery. When Maggie told her dad about her day, he'd decided they needed to leave the compound and began making arrangements for their escape. Without his mate and Maggie's mother.

"She's all in with Zachery." That was the only explanation Vixen would get.

Not that Vixen couldn't read between the lines, which she clearly did if the look Vixen shared with Bray was anything to go by.

"So, this is Mac's."

Vixen stopped in the middle of the path and nodded toward a small cabin with an old male standing in front of the door. A long beard hid the bottom of his face, but wrinkles made a map of the skin she saw. He had to be really old to have that many wrinkles as a shifter.

The old shifter pulled off his hat, revealing gray hair almost as wild as Maggie's curly brown mop. "Are you Maggie?"

She nodded.

"Bray and I are going to stay out here, but you don't have to go inside if you don't want to. We just want you to be able to speak with Mac in private."

Maggie leaned forward and peered around Bray's massive chest to look at Vixen. "Um, you know I know you can still hear us, even if we're inside, right?"

Both Bray and Mac laughed. Bray's laughter tended toward a low rumbling chuckle, similar to Finley's, but not quite the same, and Mac's was a full on high-pitched belly laugh that just missed being labeled as a cackle.

"You are no better than the boys." Vixen shook her head and looked up at the sky. "Whatever worries any of us had about you and the pack have officially been put to rest."

"Git up here, girl. We have a bit to talk about."

Maggie wanted a break from answering questions about the Gaze. Not that she minded the questions, she was just coming to hate the looks her answers almost always brought. But Vixen and Bray and–

Finley.

Yes, and Finley and the rest of the pack had been nice to Maggie, and if they only wanted her to meet an old shifter, then she'd deal with another round of looks of pity. She stuck her hands in the pockets of her borrowed pants and rubbed her thumb across the knife Finley gave her.

Finley was there. Watching her. He might not be next to her, but he hadn't left her alone. The knowledge gave her strength, and she shuffled forward, but her hand remained on the knife.

"You want to come inside or stay out here?" The old shifter asked.

"Does it matter?"

"Nope. Just a preference. Why don't we start out here and we can go inside later if yer comfortable."

"How come I think I have to recalibrate the meaning of a lot of words."

"Well, Gazes are secretive and other shifters don't know that much about them." Mac sat in a weathered Adirondack chair that was probably as old as him. "Come on, sit down or Vixen is gonna get to pacing and then we might have a whole new situation we have to deal with."

Maggie settled in the chair next to his and pulled her legs up so she sat cross-legged. "Why did she want me to meet you? And how come everyone knows who I am?"

"Well, both those questions have answers with a long story." Mac leaned back in his chair and folded his hands over his stomach. "To start, it would seem that since I took over as sentinel of the Peak, everyone who's found their way here is supposed to be here."

"I'm supposed to be here? That's why everyone knows who I am?"

"No. Everyone knows who you are because Danielle is supposed to be here."

"So, you're just not going to answer me."

"It's more difficult than a simple answer." The old shifter leaned back in his chair and laced his fingers together over his stomach. "Are you familiar with those wooden stacking dolls?"

Maggie bit down on her lip and fought against the urge to wrap her hands around the old male's throat and throttle him.

"The pack is sort of like that. If Bray hadn't had arrived at my door, then the boys wouldn't have had a place to go. Vixen's fate would have been different, Eleanor would still be struggling as a human raising a wolf shifter in a human world, and Danielle would have been disappeared somewhere." Mac pulled an old leather-bound journal from the front pocket of his overalls. "I didn't realize it until Eleanor arrived, but everyone's here for a reason. Even Bray and the boys are here because they're supposed to be."

"So you're saying I'd be here even if…"

"Vixen filled me in, yep, you'd have found your way here even if you hadn't seen something you weren't supposed to." His gnarled finger tapped against the cover of the book in his hands. "Ol' Edna was as cuckoo as a box of cocoa puffs, but she wrote about Vixen and the others, and even you more than 150 years ago in her journals. Not by name, but you're on the pages of this book."

Maggie rubbed her hand over her forehead and eyes. "None of this makes any sense."

"It never does." Mac stretched his legs out in front of him and crossed his ankles. "Broken Peak isn't named after the mountain. It's named for those who came and will come here. Before Bray and Vixen, before even me, the lost and broken have found their way here."

"Still confused."

Mac let out a long and loud sigh, just for her benefit. "You're worried that your Gaze is going to find you and try to hurt the pack, right?"

"I guess." She wasn't sure she liked how spot-on Mac was with his assessment.

"You're not bringing any more danger than the others have. And it wouldn't matter if you did, because you're supposed to be here. Just like everyone else." Mac opened the journal and flipped through the pages. When he found what he was looking for, he handed the book to her. "Read this."

Maggie looked down at the flowing script.

Great, he couldn't just spell it out for her. No, she had to read something written by a crazy shifter and divine its meaning. Maybe this pack wasn't so different from the Gaze after all. Zachery was big on referencing written works by the great leaders of before. Anything written a century ago could apply to current day, all the reader had to do was ignore all reason and logic.

A single sentinel will stand guard until the Hero, the Sage, the Mage, the Rebel, the Crown, and the Muse arrive.

There were more flowery words, but they all blurred together. She looked up at Mac. "What's it supposed to mean?"

"I believe the first four she lists are self-explainable."

"I suppose being named an rebel is preferable to a thief."

Mac tugged at the end of his beard as he studied Maggie. "Being a rebel isn't a bad thing. All the Sentinels Edna named exist outside the bounds of the rules in some way."

"Yeah, but they get titles like the Hero and the Mage. Is there even magic, though? I mean, I guess humans consider shifters magic. If they knew about us."

"Danielle is capable of pulling information out of thin air with the help of her computers. Edna and the Great Shifters didn't understand what a computer was, much less that they aren't magical."

"But the Rebel? Really?"

"Maybe Edna's translation isn't accurate, maybe the Great Shifters named you Rogue instead, but Edna was being kind."

"What? Why?"

"What's in your pockets, Maggie?"

"Nothing! Why?" Her eyes got big in the way she'd been trained since she was a kit just entering school. Deny and fake outrage. All kits learned the basic defense at an early age.

Mac laughed softly and shook his head. "Try again, Maggie. The Gazes and leaders aren't the only reasons most raccoons aren't accepted or trusted by other shifters."

"Okay, fine." Maggie blew out her breath and tilted her head to the side with her gaze averted away from Mac. Pressing her shoulders into the back of the chair until her body formed an even plane and dug her hand into her pocket. Her fist, filled with trinkets and knick-knacks from the Lodge, almost got stuck when she pulled her hand back out. With her palm up, she opened her hand and showed Mac her treasures. "I was just borrowing them. I planned on giving them back, I promise."

"And yet a covert operative for the government, one of the best, didn't even know you picked them up."

"How do you know that?" Maggie stuffed her shineys back into her pocket before lowering her bottom back to the seat of the chair.

Mac tilted his head toward Vixen and Bray. "I don't believe anyone has brought about that look of surprise on her face before."

Maggie refused to look across the way just to see the look of disappointment that was undoubtedly there. "Is she angry?"

"Nope. Knowing Vixen, she's plotting."

"We know who The Ruler is, but the time to bring her to Broken Peak isn't right yet. Vixen's been working on it, laying the foundation, and for you too if you choose to stay."

"If I choose to stay? Aren't you supposed to be convincing me this is my destiny and I have to stay?"

"Free-will still exists, Maggie. If you decide to walk away, that's your choice. But you won't just be walking away from something bigger than any of us could even begin to comprehend, you'll also be walking away from him." Mac grinned with a wink and tilted his head to the side, toward a pacing Finley who'd given up staying hidden in the shadows, but still hadn't closed the distance to join Vixen and Bray. "Regardless of what you choose, the Pack will help. If you want to leave, they'll get you and your father new identities. But they'll do it right and you'll need to be patient."

"So I can leave, but not right now?"

"You can leave now, but you'll get caught and brought back to the Gaze. I know you don't have much of a reason to trust any of us, but give us a chance, okay? If it's what you want, we'll get both you and your father to safety, but it will take some time. Vixen will have to reach out to some contacts and they have other things in motion that just can't come to a stop."

"Like the Ruler?"

"Like the Ruler." Mac agreed.

Maggie lifted her gaze and stared at Vixen. "I'm not a hero. And Gazes don't give up, ever. They attack first and ask questions later."

"I'd say you running from a Gaze knowing what they are capable of doing if they find you is very much what a hero does."

Alarms sounded in Maggie's brain. Mac was using the same tricks her father used when he needed to convince her to do what he wanted. Years with her father had created a sort of immunity to the tactic. The only weakness she had was guilt, and she didn't know anyone in Broken Peak enough to feel guilt. "I don't belong here. I belong with my father and I can't get distracted by the crazy ramblings of a crack-pot."

"The pack will help with your dad, even if you choose to walk away." Mac reached out and set his hand next to hers without actually touching her. "You don't have to go at it alone."

"Yeah, thanks, but no thanks."

CHAPTER EIGHT

MAGGIE stomped back and forth in front of the porch, her hands waving in the air like she was a flight attendant directing the passengers to the emergency exits.

"What do you think she's saying?"

"No clue."

Allard and Finley watched her performance from the front room windows since Vixen stood in front of the door and refused to let anyone outside while Maggie ranted and raved to the sky.

"Who do you think she's cursing more? You, Vixen, or Mac?"

"Me? Why would she be cursing me?"

Allard turned his head slowly and looked at Finley as though he sprouted a third head. "Really?"

"Really. I haven't done anything to her. Why'd she be cursing me?"

"Give it a minute." Allard looked back out the window.

Maggie had stopped pacing and planted her hands on her hips. Her glare landed on the window they watched from, and her brows lowered as she narrowed her eyes.

"He's not going to find the answer. The same way Leighton and Jackson didn't get it right away." Vixen glanced over from her perch where she'd been scrolling through the messages on her phone.

"I think she's calmed down enough for you to head out there and offer her some comfort." Allard patted Finley's shoulder. "Good luck."

Finley rolled his eyes and turned to Vixen. "Are you still guarding the door?"

Vixen leaned to the side and peered out the window. "Eh, I'd give her a few more minutes, but yeah, you can go out there now, I guess." She stepped away from the door and walked across the room, then down the hallway without another word.

Allard followed behind Vixen, but gave Finley another quick pat on his back before he left.

Sometimes there was no making sense of what his pack had to say, but they all had an opinion and wanted to share it. Even if he didn't care what they thought. Before his wolf lost his mind from not being able to reach Maggie, he walked out of the lodge. Instead of going right to her, he followed the porch around to the side of the house before it disappeared into the rock of the mountain.

Maggie hadn't moved. If anything, her glare had developed into a full-on glower. Maybe this is what Allard meant about needing luck. The last time he'd seen a female glower like that had been when Eleanor found out Finley told Foster Jackson was his dad. Not like the kid hadn't figured it out before Finley told him, but Eleanor had redefined the word pissed-off as Finley understood it.

He approached the porch railing and rested his forearms on them as he leaned forward. "Maggie."

"What?" She huffed out the word in a way that both Finley and his wolf found too fucking adorable for either of their own good.

"You okay?"

"No. No, I'm not okay." The waving of hands in the air with the accompanying pacing and ranting resumed. "I'm not okay. I saw a Gaze member shot. In the head! They shot him in the head. Blew his brains all over the place and I left my dad there. I left my dad there while I ran away like a coward and then Mac says I'm supposed to fulfill a prophecy or some shit. No. I am definitely not okay."

As soon as Finley heard the words shot and head, he swung his legs over the railing. His feet barely touched the ground before sprinting the few remaining feet across the yard to her. "Maggie?"

She stopped and looked up at Finley. Whatever fueled her outburst left in a rush, like what happened to Foster's toys when the batteries died. Her shoulders slumped forward as her arms dropped to her sides and she hung her head in defeat. "I left him. He'd never leave me, and I just left him alone with an entire Gaze who'd do anything Zachery said."

Finley wrapped his arms around her and pulled her in for a hug. It was what he saw his pack do with their mates when the females were upset about something. He didn't understand why it worked, but it never failed to ease Eleanor and Danielle. The hugging thing even worked with Vixen sometimes. And Vixen was not a hugger. At all.

As soon as his arms tightened around her, the crying began.

The hugging thing wasn't working. Helpless and not knowing what else to do, he spouted the first words that came to mind. "I'll do whatever you need me to do. What do you want?"

Brushing the back of her hand across her cheeks to wipe away the tears, she detangled herself from his arms and stepped away with a sniff. "Whatever I want?"

He regretted his words as soon as she asked. He might be willing to do anything, but that didn't necessarily mean he'd be able to do it. His wolf pushed closer to the surface, not at all enjoying Maggie's distress and fully on board with doing anything if it eased the little raccoon shifter. Yep, this was going right on top of the list of things he might wish he hadn't done. Like jumping into the river right after the thaw because he wanted to be first in the water. Or crossing the ice after the first freeze that didn't fully freeze the slow-moving current, so he could be the first once again. "Whatever you want. Yes."

"I need to go back to the camper."

"Okaaay?" Finley wasn't sure what answer she wanted.

"Okay." Apparently that was the answer she wanted.

Wiping the remaining tears from her cheeks, the same tears that destroyed both Finley and his wolf, she brushed his arm as she walked by him and back into the Lodge.

Shit. This wasn't good. He might have beat up those males, but he wasn't foolish enough to believe he scared them off for good. She couldn't go back to War. Not alone.

"Fine, but I'm taking you." Finley trotted after her. *And I'm gonna park in that Damn spot Danielle found us and watch you for the whole fucking time you don't have two feet firmly planted inside pack territory.*

He found her in Vixen's room shoving her book and pocket knife into the small canvas bag Finley had just pulled out of the tree earlier that day. It hadn't been twelve hours since Finley convinced the raccoon to come inside, and she was already leaving.

She hoisted the bag over her shoulder and spun around, her eyes snapping to every nook and crevice. "Where are my clothes?"

"What?" Finley pressed his hand against the door and pushed it open the rest of the way.

"My clothes. They were in the bag when I left, but they aren't here now. Where are they?" Maggie crouched down and looked under the bed, giving Finley a perfect view of her perfect ass.

Shit.

His cock punched against the zipper of his pants.

Finley wanted her. His wolf wanted her. He wanted her in his bed. In his arms. Under him, on top of him, beside him, it didn't matter as long as she wasn't anywhere else or with anyone else.

Except none of that would be possible. Not with Maggie insisting on leaving Broken Peak, and definitely not with the government still coming after the pack. The attacks had slowed, but they hadn't given up entirely. Vixen explained the decreased frequency of attempts to snatch Foster as the man in charge having other concerns and worries distracting him, but the respite wouldn't last forever and they needed to be prepared. Finley couldn't, not in good conscience, bring a mate into the pack. And that was the only way his wolf would be satisfied.

Was this what Allard had been going on about?

Shit.

The fantasy of Maggie as his mate tempted him. But only for a few seconds, and not because of anything he did to stop it.

Maggie stood in front of him, waving her hand in his face. "Hellooooo. My clothes? Do you know where they went?"

Shit. Again. How long had she been standing there and had she noticed his hard on that hadn't gone away? If anything, it was worse.

Finley's wolf sat proudly in the back of his thoughts. Perfectly fine if the female noticed.

"I'm sure they're here somewhere. Why don't we check the laundry?" Yes, checking the laundry was a reasonable suggestion. Plus, it distracted her from looking around the room and possibly catching sight of his erection. He turned and walked down the hall toward the kitchen, expecting the tiny raccoon shifter to follow behind him.

After Eleanor arrived with Foster, Vixen purchased additional washers and dryers. She'd also migrated them to a new room, off the side of the lodge where pack members claimed rooms for offices or in Danielle's case, a computer room. Eleanor had also taken over the laundry since most of the males had no issues wearing clothes until they could stand on their own. She even washed their sheets and towels, as long as the pack dumped them into one of the many hampers.

It was great having clean clothes and sheets, but Finley had no clue where the laundry room was exactly. He shortened his stride as he turned left down a hallway he only visited when invited.

Maybe Maggie wouldn't guess he didn't know where he was going?

And that particular wish wasn't coming true.

All the doors, every single one, were closed.

He closed his eyes and prayed to the moon, something he'd never done in his life, for a bit of divine inspiration.

"Whoa, I didn't realize this place is so big. It looks smaller from the front."

"It's bigger on the inside." Danielle snorted and pushed her glasses up her nose as she stepped out of her computer room.

Finley wasn't saved by divine inspiration. A human intervention bailed his ass out of appearing like an idiot.

"I was just coming to find you." Danielle closed the door to her office, preventing Maggie from seeing the bank of computers or any of the information displayed on the screens. She reached into her pocket and pulled out a phone, handing it to Maggie. "Vixen said you'd need this. But don't use it unless it's a number on the contact list. I'm working on a way for you to safely communicate with your father. Until I do, we have to assume your pack–"

"Gaze." Maggie corrected Danielle.

She took the correction in stride, "we have to assume your gaze has the means to trace calls to your dad and they can use it to find you again."

"Again? How do you know about the rest stop?" Maggie's head moved back and forth between Danielle and Finley like she was watching a tennis match.

"Rest stop?" Finley practically roared, and Maggie flinched away from him. "What happened at a rest stop, Maggie?"

"You didn't tell her about the hotel?" Danielle stared at Finley and fisted her hands on her hips while tapping her toe against the floor.

"What hotel?"

"Why didn't you tell her?"

"I'm waiting to hear about the rest stop."

Everyone spoke at once, glaring at each other in a three-way stand-off.

Finley won the glaring contest when Maggie dropped her gaze. He wasn't as worried about Danielle. Leighton could handle his mate and no way was Finley stupid enough to do anything to rile Leighton up when it came to Danielle. Leighton could be enough of a sociopath without tossing the female he and his wolf bonded with into the mix.

"Maggie," Finley tilted his head back and stared at the ceiling. "What exactly happened at the rest stop?"

He hadn't expected her to relay everything that happened, from Maggie's close call meeting with the member of her Gaze to the stranger helping her escape. By the time she finished, both Finley and his wolf were so riled, he was pacing up and down the hall and grumbling under his breath to stop himself from locking Maggie inside the Lodge and never letting her step foot outside without an armed guard. Preferably six armed guards, seven if he included Vixen.

Danielle stared at Finley with her head tilted to the side. "Okay, I think he's going to need a moment."

"What hotel?"

Maggie asked as he drew closer. Finley spun away before she could see the rage building inside of him from the memory of the three idiot males waiting in the motel parking lot for her.

"Well, I guess it's more of a motel than a hotel. And it would appear as though your pack, er Gaze, has better tech than I assumed. This adds a bit of a challenge." Danielle pressed the phone into Maggie's hand. "Yeah, so don't call anyone unless they're on the list of contacts. Not that there's many on there, just Finley, Vixen, Bray, me, and Eleanor. I used different names, but you'll figure it out."

The pacing didn't satisfy Finley's wolf. It didn't satisfy Finley either. He wanted to head straight to Hillsville, or wherever the hell Maggie was from, and rip the throats out of every member of her gaze.

"And what does all of that have to do with the hotel?"

Danielle glanced over at Finley again. "Yeah, he's going to be a while yet."

Finley stomped away before he heard Danielle's rendition and lost whatever little control he had over his animal. And his own temper, if he was being completely honest. This time he headed out the wing with the offices and paced down the bedroom hallway. By the time he returned, the look on Maggie's face almost made him turn right back around. She gawked at him with eyes nearly twice their normal size and a jaw dropped so far down, Finley worried it might have become unhinged.

He needn't have been concerned.

As soon as her brain registered his presence, she ran at him full-tilt and shoved the palms of her hands against his chest. Despite her tiny size, Maggie packed a punch and Finley's feet pedaled back a few steps before he regained his balance.

"Are you mad?" She pushed up on her toes and got her face as close to his as her five feet allowed. "You have to be certifiable to do something as stupid as going after a Gaze. They're going to come after you and bite your face off!"

Finley couldn't help the smile that appeared. He knew the little raccoon was spunky, but she had no qualms about getting right in the face of a dominant wolf and baring her, albeit small, fangs. "They weren't in Gaze territory."

"It doesn't matter." Now it was Maggie's turn to pace up and down the hallway with her arms waving over her head as she listed off a litany of even more reasons why she needed to distance herself from the pack.

"I thought she knew." Danielle didn't need to say the words that she was sorry. The tone of her voice, and the way her body hunched down when she bumped against Finley, conveyed her apology.

"She hasn't been here for even a day. When would I have had the time to share it with her? Plus, it happened over a week ago."

"You're still going to take her back to her RV?"

Finley studied the thrust of Maggie's jaw and the sway of her hips as she lengthened her stride on her approach back to them. "We can't force her to stay. Vixen's orders."

Damn, she was fierce. And devastating. As much as his wolf didn't like the idea of Maggie leaving the territory, it was for the best. He reminded himself that now wasn't the right time to take a mate. And even if the pack wasn't being attacked from all sides by the government, adding another enemy to Broken Peak's growing list wasn't for the best. Especially with a pup and humans in the mix.

"Well?"

Finley blinked. Had Maggie been talking the entire time? He blinked a second time.

Maggie rolled her eyes, as though she knew he wasn't listening, expected it even. "My clothes? Where are they?"

He sighed and looked expectantly at Danielle. She spent all of her time when she wasn't with Leighton sitting in front of her computers. She had to know the location of the laundry room.

"Um, over there." Danielle pointed to a wide-open door a few doors away from her computer room.

How had he not noticed the rumbling machines during his laps up and down the hallway? Hell, for that matter, how the hell had Maggie not noticed them either?

"Grab your clothes and let's go." He blurted out the words before he thought better. "Not that I want you to go, but it'll be dark soon."

Well, that was a particularly stupid explanation. Both Maggie and Finley could see just fine at night. Hell, she could probably see better than him.

She stood in front of him, staring with narrowed eyes and pursed lips. As if she was trying to figure Finley out. He didn't move. Not even to blink. Whatever she was looking for, she found. Or maybe she didn't, but wasn't willing to put any more energy into parsing out and deciphering his words. Maggie nodded and pivoted, walking to the laundry room with the same determination she showed during her arm waving rants.

"I'll figure out a way to safely contact your dad, but until then don't call anyone not on your contact list." Danielle escaped to her computer room before she got caught in the cross-hairs of another argument that wasn't really an argument.

Maggie stepped out of the laundry room, dressed in a pair of ill-fitting jeans and a ratty sweater. The clothes were in awful shape and Finley wondered how they hadn't fallen apart in the washer and dryer, but Maggie appeared more comfortable in them than she had in the borrowed clothes. Which had been just as ill-fitting, but at least they had been in better condition.

She dug into her pocket and pulled out the pocketknife. "Here."

"It's yours. I gave it to you. Well, your raccoon."

"You sure?"

Finley just nodded, not trusting his mouth to spit out any coherent words with the giant lump residing in his throat.

Yeah, it was all for the best that Maggie was leaving Broken Peak. At least that's what Finley tried to tell himself while simultaneously keeping his wolf from bursting free and dragging Maggie back to his room where he could keep her safe.

CHAPTER NINE

"OH, hell no." Finley pulled the Range Rover up to what was left of Maggie's RV. "You are *not* staying here."

The door to the camper had been torn off and everything that had once been inside was now strewn around the ground. Even the hood had been wrenched up and the hoses and wires ripped from the engine.

Maggie hadn't waited for Finley to come to a complete stop before she was out of the SUV and standing in the middle of her broken and destroyed belongings. She covered her face with her hands and her head fell forward until her chin hit her chest. The sobs wrenched through her body and her shoulders trembled.

Finley's wolf wanted Finley to go to her. But she needed time alone. Whether he stayed in the car or stood next to her wouldn't make a difference to what she was probably feeling and thinking at the moment.

It was only when she dropped her hands and began the tedious chore of cleaning up the mess that amounted to everything she had that Finley emerged from behind the steering wheel.

"Maggie?"

She ignored him and continued gathering the broken belongings in her arms.

"Maggie?" He tried again.

This time she turned her head toward him, but just as quickly, she resumed collecting the remnants.

He couldn't leave her to clean up the mess by herself. And he even understood her need to take her things. How many times had he moved from place to place with a black plastic sack filled with everything he owned, which wasn't much, but it was still his.

Finley reached through the window and popped the rear hatch. Using the pretense of rearranging the contents in the back, he sent a quick text back to the Pack.

We're coming back. Probably going to need Vixen and Eleanor. This Gaze shit is fucked up. All. The. Way. Fucked. Up.

He slid his phone into his pocket before anyone responded and headed back to the destruction.

Together they gathered whatever was on the ground and loaded it into the SUV. Finley didn't question her need to take a broken plate. And she didn't ask why he was helping her.

The silence between them wasn't uncomfortable though. It didn't have any of the tension that usually accompanied two people alone who weren't talking. He didn't even protest when she picked up the shredded rubber hose from the engine and shoved it into the growing pile.

Finally, when there wasn't a single trace of anything that was Maggie inside the camper or on the ground, she stopped and looked at Finley.

"Why?"

"I don't know." Finley shook his head from side to side in a slow arc. "Probably pissed at me and took it out on you. But you aren't staying here, Maggie. You know that, right?"

"I'll go to the motel."

"No, they were waiting there for you before. That's the first place they're gonna look once they figure out you've been here and seen what they did." He cut off her next destination of choice before she opened her mouth and got the words out. "You're coming back to Broken Peak. End of discussion."

Maggie turned away from him, but she hadn't surrendered. While she climbed into the front seat, she offered up her next best argument. "The Gaze will just find me there and then they'll definitely bite all your faces, and you have a pup and humans living with you. They can't defend themselves against an angry mob of raccoons."

"A, Foster did just fine scooping you up and carrying you back to the Lodge. Two, we have a Vixen and trust me when I tell you that a Vixen beats a Gaze of raccoons, even on a bad day. And D, you are coming back to Broken Peak." Finley got into the Range Rover and shifted into gear. "Put on your seatbelt. No way you wouldn't go hurling through the air if we got into an accident."

Her head listed to the side and her eyebrows pulled together over her nose as she stared at him. "None of that made any sense. You can't start with a letter, jump to a number, then skip a letter when you hop back."

But she did buckle her seatbelt and hadn't countered his argument. Finley stuck the conversation in the win column. "It's an old movie reference from the 90s. Danielle likes to watch them."

Maggie twisted in the front seat and looked into the back, reassuring herself that her things hadn't disappeared into thin air. Finley had done the same thing more times than he could count before heading into the army and getting yanked out only to be sent to Broken Peak. He totally got that compulsion despite reason telling him there was no way for things to just disappear. "I didn't see a TV anywhere, how are you all watching movies?"

"Danielle got this projector thing and declares a movie night where we have to all sit in the front room and watch." Finley pulled onto the road and headed back to Broken Peak. If luck stayed with him, he'd get Maggie back to the lodge safe and sound. But considering how fickle it had been towards Maggie, he wasn't optimistic. "I think Vixen is getting annoyed with the frequency though and might have ordered a bunch of TVs for our rooms."

"How often do you have movie nights?"

"Almost every night."

"Every night?"

"Yeah, it wasn't sold that way either. And we have to keep things G and PG rated because of Foster. Which totally sucks because just when *Let it Go* leaves your brain, someone walks back humming or singing it and you're back to constantly hearing that stupid song in your head. My wolf has even grown to hating it and he couldn't care less about music."

"Let it go?"

Finley almost drove off the side of the road. "You've never heard it?"

Maggie shook her head. "We weren't supposed to read or watch anything that wasn't approved. And my mother is so convinced by Zachery's brilliance, we never had a TV." A few seconds later, Maggie grabbed the dashboard and stared out the front windshield, like she'd seen a ghost. "My dad!"

The Range Rover's wheels swerved toward the shoulder as Finley jerked the steering wheel to the right when he turned to look at Maggie. Once free of the land of the rumble strips, Finley took a deep breath and straightened the front end of the SUV between the lines painted on the highway. He'd been wondering when Maggie was going to put the condition of her RV and her father's well-being together. He expected it sooner, but hoped it wouldn't happen until they got back to Broken Peak. Vixen and the girls were better at the comforting thing.

Finley's wolf agreed with him and sat firmly in the keep your big mouth shut camp. And Finley would have been right there with his wolf if he wasn't convinced Maggie would take a flying leap from a moving car to check on her father's welfare.

"Once we get back to the Lodge, we'll see if Danielle's made any progress. She's a whiz with things like that." They had said nothing to Maggie about what exactly Danielle did, and it wasn't Finley's place to decide what to share with Maggie. That was for Vixen and Bray, his Alphas. But at that moment, pack hierarchy landed somewhere between jack and shit. "She's fantastic with computers, Maggie. If anyone can figure out how to contact your dad and keep both of you safe, she can. In fact, she came up with the system that found you."

"What system?" She crossed her arms over her chest and turned her head to the side to better glare at Finley. "I thought it had to do with the prophecy and that old coyote."

"Really? You bought into that?" He glanced over at her before returning his eyes to the road in front of him.

She brushed his change of topic away with a wave of her hand. "What system, Finley."

Finley closed his eyes for a moment and began counting to ten before remembering he was driving and opened his eyes. "Danielle built a program that looks for things and apparently what was happening to you was one of those things it looked for."

"Yeah, I'm gonna need more information than that."

"Well, good news then, you can ask Danielle exactly how it works once we get back to the Lodge." Finley flashed a grin at her and turned off the highway onto the logging road that would bring them back to Broken Peak and the safety of the Pack. "And you'll have plenty of time to get all the answers you want because you aren't going anywhere until you and your father have a new identity and I know you'll be safe."

Finley said that last bit under his breath. Not quiet enough for her not to hear, but at least Maggie didn't argue with him.

Both Finley and his wolf placed her lack of argument firmly in the winning column.

Yeah for him.

CHAPTER TEN

AS a whole, the pack had been welcoming. Once Finley brought Maggie back to the house, Eleanor had swept her away and led Maggie to a spare bedroom. After countless apologies for giving Maggie a bedroom without a bathroom and making Maggie promise over and over she wouldn't hesitate to ask for anything, Eleanor finally left her alone.

Except Maggie wasn't alone. Finley parked himself right outside her door. When she woke up the next morning, if what she had done during the night even qualified as sleep, and opened the bedroom door to go to the bathroom, she tripped over his wolf.

Sure, she'd never seen his wolf before, but there was no mistaking the shocking blue color, nearly turquoise, of his eyes. That his wolf's eyes weren't more similar to a wild wolf's was a bit of a surprise. There had been a few members in the Gaze with lighter-colored eyes, but all their raccoons had the similar brown eyes.

After she had righted herself, the wolf stood and stretched, lowering the front half of his body while keeping the back half upright. He wagged his tail in a slow satisfied manner and sauntered down the hallway, clearly convinced he was the only reason she was still breathing.

She showered, brushed her teeth, and completed all the requisite morning hygiene rituals, then Maggie hunted down Danielle. The human female hadn't been difficult to find. She was locked behind a door that hid the bank of computers Finley hinted at the day before while driving back to Broken Peak.

Though Danielle hadn't allowed Maggie to talk with her dad, she got to see pictures and read a detailed report. Her father didn't look well, but he also didn't look beaten. Apparently, Vixen was well-connected and found someone to keep an eye on Maggie's father. Whoever was watching her dad was under strict orders to call Vixen if anything changed at the compound in Moundsville. Or that's what Danielle promised Maggie before stepping back into the room and closing the door in Maggie's face.

At least she got to keep the picture. She folded it up, careful not to crease her dad's face, and stuck it in her pocket next to the knife.

And that left her in the current predicament. Maggie was an outsider to the pack and while they were all polite and friendly, they didn't trust her. Not that she blamed them. Raccoon shifters didn't have a sterling reputation in the shifter world. And not because the other shifters were prejudiced. The raccoons had earned every single mark against them.

Without having anything better to do, Maggie headed toward the front room. She had promised Vixen, Bray, and Finley she wouldn't leave the Pack's territory, but as far as she understood, pack territory didn't start at the front porch. The first snow hadn't fallen yet, and even though it was cooler in Virginia in the first week of December, the weather was still pleasant enough to spend time outside.

As soon as she stepped outside, Eleanor looked over at Maggie from her perch on the porch swing. The human female's eyebrows shot up in surprise when she discovered it was Maggie who joined them and not someone else from the Pack.

"Oh…" Eleanor had an odd expression of panic combined with confusion.

Maggie didn't leave Eleanor in suspense for long as she sat down on the swing next to the human. "Don't worry. I'm not making a break for it. There wasn't anything for me to do inside."

Eleanor raised her coffee mug toward the yard. More specifically, to Foster, who was running from random spot to random spot picking up things. "We're collecting flora."

"This late?"

"Sometimes we can't spend much time outside, so when we can, I try to come up with projects I can justify as being somewhat educational."

Maggie leaned back in the swing and pulled her legs up so she was sitting cross-legged. A dull ache throbbed in her stomach. Her mother hadn't ever done anything remotely close to creating a project to keep Maggie entertained. If Maggie couldn't help increase her mother's standing with Zachery, she forgot about her daughter.

Foster stopped his leaf collecting and looked up from his scrutiny of the ground. "Can you climb trees?"

The pup's innocent question yanked her right out of a round of self-pity that wouldn't solve anything except make her envious that she didn't have the type of childhood Foster, or probably most of the Pack, had. "Yeah, I can."

"So can I." Foster walked closer to the porch. "Can you climb down trees?"

"Yep. I can do that too. If I couldn't, I'd still be up in a tree right now, wouldn't I?"

He considered her logic with a slight tilt of his head and another step closer to the porch. "I guess. But I have uncles who help me down. Do you have uncles helping you?"

"No. No uncles. Just me." Maggie would answer all the questions Foster asked if it meant she avoided answering the questions Eleanor looked ready to ask. In her experience, questions from curious grown-ups were always worse than questions from curious young.

"I bet Uncle Finley would help you. His wolf wouldn't let me visit you this morning." Foster hopped back to his investigation after leaving that particular bombshell in his wake.

Eleanor covered her face with her palm and shook her head. "I'm so sorry. I should have warned you to lock the door. Foster has a strict open door policy when it comes to unlocked doors." She tilted her head and peeked out from between her fingers. "Uncle Finley's wolf, huh? He must really like you. Usually he gives in when it comes to Foster and his wants."

Maggie ignored the question because it wasn't really a question, something she learned early on in her life at the Gaze. Don't answer anything but direct questions and only answer what's asked. It usually pissed off the high-ranking gaze members, but technically, she wasn't being insubordinate when she said yes to whether she knew the time. She stood from the swing and walked to the porch railing. Leaning against it, she watched Foster scamper from one spot to another.

From the fluttering of Eleanor's eyebrows, the human was getting ready to pounce with another question. Foster might be Maggie's ticket to putting off any awkward questions she wasn't ready to answer. Even if her raccoon hadn't stopped singing her rendition of the mine song since seeing Finley in front of her door this morning.

"Foster?"

The pup picked his head up from the ground and turned his face to her. "Yeah?"

"Can you wag your tail?"

"Yeah, silly. Can't you?"

Maggie shook her head. "Not really. I can sort of move it and it helps me with balance, but I never learned how to wag it."

A quick glance over her shoulder revealed Eleanor still had the calculating look of someone waiting for the exact right moment to pounce. Maybe Maggie could delay the inevitable with Foster's help.

"How do you wag your tail, Foster?"

His head bounced from side to side as he considered the question. Before Maggie knew what was happening, Foster had his bottom stuck out behind him while he wiggled.

"Nope. That's not it." Foster jumped to the side, bottom still out since he was bent slightly forward, and gave another shake. "That's not it. One sec and I'll get it."

And then Foster was hopping around in a circle, shaking his bottom in all manner of different ways in what must have been an attempt at figuring out just how he wagged his tail. Maggie's plan not only backfired, it went up in a giant poof of smoke.

She could have found another diversion, but sometimes it was better to face whatever the issue head on. This was going to be one of those times, Maggie just knew it. The two human women, and whatever the hell Vixen was, seemed to have a tenacity that would drive them to the ends of the earth to get an answer to their question.

"I can't mate. I mean I can, it's not that I'm physically unable. It's more that I'm not in a position to mate. With anyone." Maggie turned and leaned back against the railing so she was looking at Eleanor instead of Foster.

Eleanor had the decency to blush while she hid most of her face behind her coffee mug. "Oh. I didn't. I wasn't. I don't..."

After a bit more stumbling over words, Maggie saved Eleanor. "You were curious, I get it. If I grew up in one of the common houses like my mother wanted instead of the house my father insisted on, I'd be just as curious if a Gaze member showed interest in someone who didn't live with us."

"I guess I didn't expect such a direct answer. Between the way I danced around Jackson, and then Leighton and Danielle had their own river of denial…" Eleanor stopped rambling and looked down at her sock-covered toes as she wrangled her thoughts back in order. "Both Danielle and I are human and we forget that a shifter, even a raccoon shifter, would know more than we did."

Guilt landed squarely on Maggie's chest. She should have saved Eleanor sooner. And been a lot nicer. And more understanding. And the list went on. In her defense, life with the Gaze taught Maggie to always be on the lookout for an attack from any direction, even if the coast appeared clear and the question seemed innocent.

"Gazes and Gaze leaders aren't anything to mess with. I wasn't joking when I told Finley they'd bite his face off. And it wouldn't be fair to my mate, because I refuse to bring kits into a world where the Gaze could claim them. Plus, what about my dad? Once it's safe for him to leave the Gaze, I will drag him away from Zachery and my mom." She shrugged her shoulders and offered Eleanor a tiny smile. It was what it was, and she didn't want pity. "That's too much baggage to ask someone else to help carry."

"But Danielle's working on a new identity for you. And your father. Vixen says she's great at it too."

"Even if Danielle comes up with new identities and we're halfway around the world from here, the other Gazes will be watching for us. I'll always be looking over my shoulder for a Gaze enforcer. Or worse, a fanatic. At least the enforcers don't buy into the whole Zachery as the next coming of Argenti." Maggie bit down on the corner of her lip and pulled it between her teeth. Before she got too lost in the thoughts of what might have been, she pushed them away. "I couldn't do that to Finley."

"For what it's worth, Broken Peak wasn't for me, Vixen, or Danielle either, but we're all still here. You never know what will happen until it does." Eleanor stared down into the depths of her coffee mug. "Danielle keeps trying to convince me to change my hair color, add some purple or blue to it."

Okaaaay, so the complete change of topic was unexpected, even if it was welcome. Maggie was prepared to go another round. Or ten. Even her dad took her on multiple rounds when he wanted her agreement on some of the more distasteful Gaze traditions.

When Maggie didn't respond, Eleanor tried again. "Ever think about coloring your hair?"

Maggie wondered where this line of questioning was headed. As far as she could tell, she had two choices. Walk back inside and find something to do until the boredom killed her, and she came back outside for another round of questioning. Or stay put and face whatever it was Eleanor was hinting at without the boredom break.

The latter of the two seemed to be the best option. Maggie plopped back in the swing and scooted along the seat until her shoulders hit the back. It was the most comfortable way to sit on the worn wood. Of course, this also meant her feet didn't even come close to touching the ground. The bane of short legs. "Not really. But it'd be kinda fun."

"Don't tell Danielle that."

"Don't tell Danielle what?" Danielle stepped out onto the porch and closed the door behind her.

"Speak of the devil." Eleanor moved over on the swing and patted the now empty space between Eleanor and Maggie. "Whacha got there?"

The distraction was enough, and Danielle settled between the two while opening the laptop computer. "Clothes. We need to get Maggie her own clothes."

"Really, I don't need anything."

The human women ignored Maggie, like she hadn't said a word, and bent their heads together. If the sound of the mouse clicking was anything to go by, Maggie wondered if they were buying new wardrobes for the entire pack. But every time she looked over and tried to gauge the contents of the online shopping cart, they switched pages so she couldn't see anything.

"I figured it out!" Foster shouted from the yard.

Any excuse to walk away from what was fast turning into a spending spree that Maggie was going to have to find a polite reason to decline was fine by her. She hopped off the swing and jogged across the lawn towards him. "Figured what out?"

"How I wag my tail." Foster proceeded to jump from foot to foot in a convoluted combination of steps. And he did all of this with his arms in the air over his head and his bottom sticking out. "See?"

Maggie didn't, but hopping around from foot to foot looking like a fool seemed more fun than watching the two humans go shopping through a computer screen.

Thirty minutes later and she was hopping around, just like Foster. She wasn't sure how the movements would transfer to her animal wagging her tail, but Foster was happy. And so was she.

CHAPTER ELEVEN

WHAT *the...* Finley stood in front of the window and stared out into the yard. Gaping was more like it if his wolf's sudden interest was anything to go by. Good thing none of his packmates were around to witness the spectacle since he'd have to kill them for seeing Maggie hopping around with her perfect ass wiggling around and making a perfect target for any wandering eye.

He'd been looking for Maggie, not too hard so it would be perfectly natural when he bumped into her, but couldn't find her anywhere in the Lodge. When he also couldn't find any of the women or Foster, he figured they were together. He just hadn't figured on Foster and Maggie doing their own thing while the women sat back and watched.

A quick calculation and Finley figured that the chance of any the males accidentally stumbling on the goings-on in the front yard was low.

He stepped outside and closed the door behind him with a soft click. The last thing he wanted was for Maggie to stop.

Yeah. He got the whole hypocrite thing going on with not wanting his packmates to see Maggie, but wanting to take in his fill of her. He pushed that little quandary aside for later. Like never. His wolf agreed so completely, Finley wondered what the hell happened to his wolf. He never agreed with Finley, just on principle.

"Uncle Finley!" Foster waved, but didn't stop dancing. "I'm teaching Maggie how to wag her tail!"

"Are you, now?" Finley took a step toward the front steps and leaned his shoulder against the column supporting the porch roof.

"Yeah. Wanna help?"

He wanted to help do a lot of things with Maggie, but he wasn't sure hopping around was top of the list.

Except...

Maggie's tongue stuck out of the corner of her mouth and tiny creases formed between her eyebrows while she concentrated on the steps her feet made. Everything about the female, so tiny she could fit in his pocket, pushed him to saying yes. If it gave him more chances to see his Pocket make those faces and wiggle her body around, he was all for it.

"Sure, kid, why not?"

"Yeah!" Foster might have jumped in excitement at the prospect of his uncle helping. Or he might have been doing part of the dance. "Let me show you how."

And that was how Finley spent the next twenty minutes. Hopping around with his arms flailing and his ass sticking out. It was a decidedly good thing that none of his packmates stumbled across the spectacle.

"Foster, come on bud, we need a bath before dinner." Eleanor called from the front porch and interrupted what had come to be called the butt dance.

The dance got its name mostly because Jackson would beat the shit out of Finley for calling it the shake your ass dance and driving Eleanor insane as she tried to keep Foster from singing about the ass dance. Also the kid laughed like a deranged lunatic whenever they called it the butt dance and then Maggie giggled. And Finley really enjoyed that particular sound coming from her. He didn't think she had much reason to giggle and laugh, and Finley wanted to change that.

"Aw, Mom!" Foster had shifted from calling Eleanor Mommy to Mom and she hated it. A few weeks ago she spent over an hour drinking wine and complaining about the new name to Finley.

Finley leaned toward Foster and gave him a gentle bump, a modified version of what the males did to one another. "Hey, bud?"

"Yeah?" He looked between his mother and uncle Finley, as though Finley might be capable of sparing him from the dreaded bath.

"Do me a favor and call your mom, Mommy tonight." Finley winked down at Foster and patted the top of his head. "And after dinner, we can ask Danielle if we can play with Hampstead."

Foster thought about it for a few moments before nodding in agreement. "Okay. Coming, Mommy!" He ran back to the porch, knees pumping high and arms swinging wildly.

Eleanor gave Finley a wave, then ushered both Foster and Danielle back inside the Lodge, leaving Finley and Maggie alone.

All alone.

Which felt kind of weird, even though it shouldn't because Finley and Maggie had spent a lot of time alone driving to War and back. Except now Finley wasn't concerned about Maggie getting jumped in her RV by some rando crazies from her Gaze. And he wasn't worried she'd run off. For the first time since the little raccoon shifter showed up at the Pack's door, Finley wasn't sure what to do or say around the female. When he chanced looking at her, wondering what he should do, Maggie was staring at him with a goofy grin on her face.

"You're cute with him."

"I'm not cute. Dominant wolves aren't cute." He grinned back at her.

"I suppose if we continue to hop around in circles without Foster, your pack will think we're both a little crazy."

"They already know I'm crazy, so I can't say hopping around like a fool is going to change their impression of me. However, I don't enjoy the prospect of the mocking I'd receive."

"Eleanor and Danielle won't tell them?"

From anyone else, Maggie's question would have been innocent, but there was a darkness lingering behind her words and it raised the hair on the back of Finley's neck and his wolf's hackles. "No, Pocket, they won't. If I had done something to annoy Eleanor, then she might have taken a picture or video of us and saved it for a later date to use as ammunition, but naw, she's not like that. None of us are."

"Pocket?" Maggie combed her fingers through her hair and pulled the curly strands back into a tight pony tail before dropping her hands and letting the curls bounce back into place. "Did you just call me Pocket?"

Shit, he'd actually called her Pocket. Yeah, he might have been thinking she'd fit in his pocket, and maybe he also started calling her Pocket in his mind. It was all Eleanor's fault. If she hadn't mentioned that Maggie would fit into anyone's pocket the idea wouldn't have firmly planted its roots in Finley's brain.

"Yeah, I guess I did." Finley ducked his head and shoved his hands into his pockets. "Sorry, must have been because we were talking about Eleanor."

Maggie lifted an eyebrow and cocked her head to the side. Yeah, he didn't buy it either.

The good news was that Maggie then changed the subject. The bad news was what she changed the subject to. "Why are you so sure none of your pack will race back and tell your Alphas?"

"Besides Vixen and Bray honestly not giving a fuck?"

"They don't?"

"Why would they care what we were doing on our time off? As long as we're doing our jobs?"

"What are your jobs here?" She looked around the yard, as if seeing it for the first time. "I mean, ya'll have lots of food and clothes and the means to buy them. And I know you have a lot of cars. I've seen them. And that big shiny coffee maker in the kitchen."

Of course she'd noticed Danielle's espresso maker. That monstrosity was too bright and shiny and had too much chrome for her not to mention it. "I guess you could say our jobs are to keep the pack safe, so we patrol the territory and with Danielle's help, stop anyone from getting too close, unless we want them there."

"Yeah, okay, but how do y'all make money to buy the things you need?"

Finley peered down at her, "you serious?"

Maggie nodded, then stepped back. Away from him. Neither Finley nor his wolf liked that she backed away, just out of arm's reach. Like she knew just where to stand to keep safe. He shoved his hands deeper in his pockets and hunched forward with his head lowered to appear smaller. Not that it would work, but it might make her a little less gun shy.

"Come on, I'll answer all your questions inside." He lifted his chin toward the front porch. "Not that I won't answer them outside either, but I feel kinda like an idiot standing out here."

"I suppose." Maggie shrugged and led the way back to the Lodge.

Finley raced up the porch steps and opened the door for her before her hand even reached the handle. They didn't need to do an awkward dance of turning this way and that since Maggie walked under his outstretched arm without having to duck.

Yep, Eleanor had definitely been right about Maggie fitting into their pockets.

"Wanna sit here?" Finley bent his head at the huge couch that, despite its ability to seat three of the big males of the pack, still looked small in the large room.

Maggie didn't answer. Instead she bit down on her lip and pulled her arms snug to her sides.

"Or we could go to the kitchen?" Maybe Finley would have to resort to bribing her with Oreos again.

"Your room?"

Well, if that little question didn't knock Finley right off his feet. Sure, he and his wolf might have imagined a number of different ways to get her into his room, but none of them included Maggie making the offer herself. "My room?"

"Unless…" Maggie sucked her bottom lip between her teeth and looked away.

Shit. Finley wanted to pull her lip free, preferably with his teeth. Well, more exactly, his wolf wanted to. With that combination of tiny gestures, all the reasons why keeping his distance from Maggie, mostly to keep his wolf from growing any closer to the little female, went out the window.

"Your room's fine." Finley waited for Maggie to lead the way. He told himself he was being polite, but it was obvious enough to anyone with half a brain cell, Finley wanted to watch the cute swivel of her hips and the adorable sway of her ass.

Was it possible for anyone, shifter or human, to have such a perfect ass? And why was this particular ass so Damn enticing when none of the many other posteriors he had seen earned more than a passing glance?

Once inside her room, with the door firmly closed and locked to keep Foster from barreling in, Finley stood in between the bed and the door, not sure what to do or say. The bed loomed large in the center of the bedroom. A bedroom bereft of anything personal, except for the small cloth bag resting on the small dresser. A dresser painfully empty since nothing they brought back from the camper had been salvageable.

The women had wanted to toss everything, but Finley, with help from Leighton, intervened. Instead of dumping the ruined items in the garbage, Finley and Leighton packed them into boxes and carefully listed the contents on the outside.

"So, um, what do you want to know about the pack?" Finley asked.

Maggie busied herself with brushing the non-existent dust particles off the top of the dresser. Once her hands couldn't find anything more to do, she reached into her pocket. But she didn't pull anything out, instead she kept her hand tucked in her pocket when she finally turned around to face him. "Everything. Anything you can share."

"There's not much I can't share. And most of what I can't share isn't about keeping things secret, they just aren't my secrets."

The words didn't make any sense to her if the way she cocked her head to the side and her forehead creased with wrinkles was anything to go by.

Finley took a breath and tried again. "So, let's say you shared something with Vixen, your middle name for example."

"I don't have one."

Finley had a brief flash of what it must have been like for Bray when a bunch of unruly adolescents rolled up to his door one after another. He made a mental note to thank Bray for not killing them all. "Let's say you do."

"But I–"

"For this example you do." Yep, Finley had to hunt down Bray and thank his Alpha for not coming up with new and exciting ways to get rid of rowdy dominant males. "You tell Vixen your middle name, but she won't tell us because it's none of her business. And if you tell Foster your favorite color, well no, actually, Foster isn't great at keeping secrets. So, instead of Foster, you tell Eleanor your favorite color and she won't share it. Unless the survival of the Pack depended on Vixen or Bray knowing what your favorite color is."

"Turquoise."

"What?"

"My favorite color. It used to be green, but now it's turquoise."

Finley grinned. He couldn't help himself. Both he and his wolf shared the same color eyes. Or maybe the wolf just made his blue eyes brighter, but ever since he'd been a little kid moving from foster home to group home to foster home, every human he ran into focused on the color of his eyes for several minutes before moving on to getting Finley settled.

He shook his head and got back to the task of explaining the ins and outs of a pack. "Leighton knows about Gazes, but he hasn't shared any specifics with us. It's your story to tell when you want to. Except if they show up here."

"When."

"What? I don't know, it's a hypothesis thing. One of those weird games Vixen and Mac play with Danielle sometimes. Figuring out all the ifs so they're prepared."

"No, I mean when they show up here. It's not an if, it's a when."

"We'll see." Some of the Gaze might show up in Pack territory, but they weren't getting close enough for Maggie to find out about it. Not if he had anything to do about it. Even if he had to sit in front of Danielle's computers twenty-four seven.

"Okaaaay." Maggie shuffled along the floor to the bed and sat down on the edge. "But how does the pack make money?"

"It's actually not that special or a big secret." Finley plopped down on the bed next to her, but not too close. "We're all a bunch of fuck ups and the packs created a trust so Bray didn't have to worry about working while he did his best to keep us from killing each other."

"Whoa. I didn't know wolves were rich. Better not let the Gaze leaders find out, or your Alphas will be fending off a bunch of females and having to lock away the adolescent and young adult males."

Finley wanted to ask more about her admission, but didn't want to spook her. He enjoyed their conversation too much to risk her clamming up. He'd remember to ask Leighton about it later, though.

"We aren't that rich. Bray is good with investments. And Vixen has money stashed all over the country. Probably the world."

"Stashes? She's not a raccoon shifter."

"It's a throwback to her old job, before she came here."

"What was her old job?"

"That's Vixen's story to share." He could have shared with Maggie, Vixen probably wouldn't have minded. But telling Maggie Vixen's story wouldn't have earned him Maggie's trust. He turned toward her with an enormous smile and hoped it would be enough to soften the blow of his refusal.

Maggie lifted her head at the same time and their lips brushed.

Finley should have pulled away.

But he didn't.

Finley definitely should have pulled away then. Especially because Maggie hesitated. She didn't pull away or push him back, but the small hitch in her breath and the timid trembling of her shoulders hinted at a level of unsureness.

But he definitely didn't.

When her lips finally parted and their tongues met, whatever held her back melted away.

She wrapped her arms around his neck and all the reasons why Finley shouldn't be kissing Maggie flew from his brain. Probably because his blood was no longer going to his brain. Instead, it headed along a direct path straight to his cock, which pressed impatiently against the fly of his jeans.

While Finley struggled with his cock's insistence on a more intimate introduction to the delightful female, the female in question had released her strangle hold on Finley's neck, but clutched her fingers in his hair.

He wanted to do more. His wolf wanted to do more. But the little voice in the back of his head, the one he first started listening to when Vixen joined their pack, told him it wasn't the right time for more.

Kisses shouldn't be so good.

By the time his mind gained a modicum of reason and his wolf was safely tucked away where he wouldn't cause additional problems by claiming the little raccoon shifter, he was already in over his head.

Oh, Finley planned on claiming her. Eventually. After the brief taste of his Pocket, he wasn't letting her go. And he sure as hell wasn't letting anyone *else* claim her.

But that could wait.

It would have to wait.

Finley pulled away from her, pressing his lips to her forehead as he did. "I'm sorry. I shouldn't have done that."

CHAPTER TWELVE

"I'M sorry. I shouldn't have done that." Finley pulled away from her, putting as much space between them as possible without getting off the bed.

Maggie's body followed his retreat. His words hadn't hit her fully just yet. It was hard to think about what he was saying when her raccoon was urging her to climb him like a tree and kiss him right back.

Not that she needed much convincing.

But when the kissing stopped and oxygen returned to her brain, Finley's words hit her straight on and nearly knocked her off her feet. And not in the good way either.

That was fine, though. She wasn't planning on staying, and Finley added a complication she wasn't certain was worth the cost. She lifted her arm and started to brush the back of her hand across her lips, but stopped herself at the last minute.

She didn't want to wipe Finley away. No matter where the should and should nots landed on his arbitrary list, Finley's kiss was something she wanted to remember.

"Don't be sorry you kissed me." Maggie looked anywhere but at him. The storm of feelings and emotions she'd never allowed herself to experience before threatened to break free and erupt. All while learning the reason for the overwhelming emotions was sorry and shouldn't have done it. His exact words, too. The last person she wanted witnessing her breakdown was the male who caused it with a kiss and then a retraction.

He'd probably kissed a bunch of females before, which was how he knew it was all a mistake.

She hadn't kissed anyone before that moment. Male or female.

Finley was her first kiss.

Ever.

And he thought it was a mistake.

"I'm not sorry I kissed you." Finley's rough fingers brushed against her chin, lifting her face so she couldn't look anywhere except at him. "I plan on kissing you again."

"You do?" Okay, so that wasn't the most romantic thing to come out of her mouth, but in all fairness, she'd never had to worry about romantic words and whispered sweet-nothings in the Gaze.

Finley nodded and pressed the pad of his thumb against her bottom lip while staring at her mouth as if it was a meal he planned on eating for breakfast, lunch, and dinner. "Pocket?"

His whisper sent a wave of warm air across her skin and she closed her eyes as his breath caressed her the way she wanted his fingers to touch her. His voice so easily captured both her and her raccoon's attention, she didn't realize he didn't use her name. "Yessss?"

"Baby, open your eyes and look at me." The rough timbre of his voice hid the barest hint of laughter.

What? Oh, yeah, her eyes. She needed to open them. She wasn't sure why and didn't really care, except Finley told her to and her raccoon was threatening to push closer to the surface and open her eyes for her. "Yeah?"

Oh. There were those turquoise eyes that almost seemed to glow. She wanted to mention something about keeping his eyes close to her, but even her raccoon vetoed that particular outburst. She didn't really want to keep his eyes close. Just the color. Her new favorite color.

Finley grinned. "Your new favorite color?"

Crapsicles. She said all that out loud.

"Yeah, you did, Pocket."

Crapsicles.

She did it again.

Before anything else left her mouth without going through her filter first, she slapped her hand over her lips.

Finley threw his head back and laughed. The sound was like a wholly unfamiliar song, but an immediate favorite when heard for the first time. The Gaze had plenty of laughter, but the noise that came from her fellow shifters was forced and their sound wasn't nearly as genuine or pretty to listen to.

He fell back on her bed, but wrapped his arm around her shoulders and brought her with him. Just like he had tucked her raccoon in his arm, Finley tucked her against his body. His rather large body.

Sure, Maggie was small, even by most raccoon shifter standards, but compared to Finley, she felt like a miniature figure created to fit inside doll houses.

His fingertips trailed down her arms and over her hip, then up her back and shoulder where they began the cycle over. Sparks traveled along her skin and woke the butterflies that lived in her stomach. They took flight, and she enjoyed that their presence signified a pleasant moment instead of a cue it was time to fight or take flight.

"Maggie?" Finley turned his head and brushed his lips across her forehead.

She tilted her head back and looked up at him, waiting for his next question. When it didn't come right away, the butterflies took flight again, but this time a wave of trepidation accompanied them.

What if–

"Pocket, I need to know that you're on board with this and whatever this is, and not using it as a distraction from the current shit show."

Her worries disappeared, and the trepidation slid away.

"This?" She swallowed back the nerves from inexperience. For over twenty years, Maggie employed every tactic, with the help of her father, to stay clear of the males in the Gaze who had Zachery's ear and could force a mating. The only problem was, it meant she'd never spent any time with any males.

"Yeah. The kiss and the things that happen after." His arm tightened around her, pulling her closer to him.

The natural response, or at least what felt like the natural response, was to swing her leg and arm over his body. Except, natural had scampered off to play with other things, leaving Maggie to figure things out on her own. In the end, she placed her arms in front of her, straight down with her hands clasped and her wrists crossed. On the comfort scale, the position fell somewhere higher than a bed of nails, but lower than a plywood board.

Finley watched her contortions in bemusement. His confusion was easy to read with his head tilted to the side and his eyes halfway closed while he turned his entire body to face her. Which put her hands right in front of his dick and Maggie scared to death of moving in case she accidentally brushed up against it.

Everything that happened since she announced her new favorite color was awkward enough without adding her breaking out into embarrassed giggles, thank you very much.

"Pocket?" Finley brushed away the stray strands of hair that fell across her face, which she couldn't do on her own without moving her arms, which she couldn't do without risking brushing her hands against his crotch.

When his steady stare caught her fleeting glances at any and everything except Finley, something inside her settled. It might have been the influence of her raccoon, or maybe it was his eyes.

His magical turquoise eyes.

Maggie swallowed back her groan. She really needed to learn not to think those thoughts until she got her brain under control enough not to say them aloud.

Finley didn't move his eyes from hers and the hunger she saw lurking just beneath the surface, excited her. In a good way. But the excitement couldn't quell her lack of experience and the insecurities that accompanied the anticipation in his stare, and she wrapped her arms around her middle.

"Don't do that, Pocket. Don't hide yourself from me."

Her arms returned to their previously awkward position between their bodies, and she ducked her head to the side.

His warm hands pressed against her cheeks and turned her face so she was looking at him once more. The turquoise eyes glowed with his wolf's presence, and her brown eyes probably flashed amber as her raccoon pushed closer to the surface. The furry monster wanted out and wanted to meet Finley's wolf, but that couldn't happen. The animal side of shifters had been known to take matters into their own paws and claim their mates while they had control.

Maggie wasn't willing to risk an accidental claiming.

Finley's thumbs brushed across the freckles on her cheeks and he smiled at her. Not a grin or a smirk, but a genuine smile. Whether it was for her raccoon's appearance or her didn't matter at the moment. The only thing she cared about was the smile. It was better than reading a book in an empty field during the summer months with the sun warming her skin, which topped the list of her top ten perfect days.

She didn't know what to do or how to do it, but the smile erased the unknown and she brought her hands up to his arms, resting them on his shoulders. Turned out it was only slightly less awkward than the earlier position, but once she touched him, she couldn't pull away. More accurately, her raccoon would allow her to pull away.

Sneaky beast.

"I'll always want to see you, Pocket. No matter what."

The magic of the moment left with the sound of his voice breaking her daydream and Maggie rolled onto her back, away from him. Finley didn't get frustrated or angry. He rolled on his back and slid over until there was a comfortable space between them. Their arms down on the bed between them, their hands close, but not quite touching.

They talked about her life with the Gaze and his life of not knowing his parents, or shifters, and moving through human foster families and group homes when his wolf became too difficult to control. Topics that would inevitably lead to Maggie's current circumstance and what she witnessed were carefully avoided.

She explained the ins and outs of Zachary's leadership and his insistence on approving all matings, even going as far as arranging the matings. It was how her dad and mother ended up together. Zachery ordered their pairing.

More than twenty years later and their bond was strong enough to cause death if broken. Her mother was enthralled with Zachery, so much she stuck a picture of him on the ceiling above her parents' bed.

Zachery's picture wasn't the reason Maggie and her dad planned on running, but Zachery was.

"I can't just leave him there. Zachery might not kill him because of the bond with my mother, but Zachery will have no qualms with torture." Maggie admitted far more than planned.

"You have the entire pack behind you. We'll help get your father free of the Gaze."

"It's not safe." She offered the same excuse she'd given before, except less emphatically this time.

"Yeah, in case you haven't figured it out yet, our pack doesn't make decisions based on how safe something is." Finley pinched her chin and tilted her face up until his gaze pinned her in place. "I'll get your dad out of there, Pocket, I promise."

Maggie's raccoon insisted she trust Finley's word, even though every experience in her relatively short life screamed that her father was the only one she could trust. Swallowing back the lump in her throat and blinking back her tears, she needed to move away from the subject of her dad.

The topic jumped to favorite books, *The Source* for Maggie and *Pete the Cat* for Finley. Then on to biggest pet peeves, both claimed noisy eaters. It was easy to talk with Finley and with everything else being difficult and complicated, both Maggie and her raccoon relished the peacefulness that settled over them.

The words they spoke didn't matter as long as he was next to her.

"This day easily makes my top ten."

"Top ten what?" Finley asked.

"Top ten perfect days. I'd say it's close to breaking the top five."

"We'll have to add more days to your list."

And with that single statement from him, Maggie and her raccoon came to an agreement. She wanted to mate and bond with Finley.

Maybe not right then, or even in a few weeks. But eventually, when Maggie's world settled down, she would find Finley and claim him.

The plan came with a hitch, though. In the meantime, Finley might find someone else.

She ignored the hitch.

She was going to bond with Finley and become his mate.

Barely an hour passed since their first kiss.

Her first kiss.

But shifters were quick that way. Their animals pointed out the obvious, and no one had to perform the complicated relationship rituals the humans seemed to enjoy. No self-doubt. No hesitation. No second-guessing.

It was what it was. Finley was Maggie's mate.

CHAPTER THIRTEEN

BRAY stood back from the others and surveyed the almost completed construction project the pack had been working on since breakfast. Vixen got it into her head she wanted a bird feeder in the yard close enough to the porch to watch the birds, but far enough away to keep the birds from flying off as soon as Vixen got close. Apparently they freaked the hell out whenever she got close, in either form.

"Are you sure it will hold? Because if it begins lilting during the winter, we'll be out in the snow fixing it."

"Lilting?" Tevin dropped his arms to the side and stared at Bray. Well, not stare as much as gape. "What the hell kind of word is lilting and why the fuck are you using it?"

Jackson pressed his hands against Foster's ears and glowered at Tevin. "Hey. Language."

"The pup's heard worse." Leighton rolled his eyes and crossed his arms over his chest. "From your own mouth too."

"Yeah, but you don't have to deal with an angry El." Jackson's hands remained covering Foster's ears. For good reason too. The pup repeated back everything he heard to his mom, and they had all been on the receiving end of a lecture from Eleanor about how impressionable Foster was.

Finley glanced down at Jackson's hands and the way they engulfed Foster's head. "Maybe we should get a set of earmuffs for the pup?"

"Hold up. Are we just passing by the whole lilting thing?" Tevin cracked a grin at Bray. "I'm fine with that, as long as we can agree to circle back at a later time."

Allard's hand came out and smacked the back of Tevin's head. "You can thank me later."

"Ow." Tevin dropped the sledge hammer in his hand and pounced on Allard, pulling him to the ground where they immediately alternated putting each other in choke holds.

Bray pressed his palm against the side of his face and shook his head slowly from side to side. "You'd think with mating and Vixen, the bunch of you would be better behaved."

"He dropped the hammer didn't he?"

"I guess it's a small improvement." Bray shrugged.

"It will take time for the cement to cure, but we stuck it two feet in the ground and it's quick set concrete." Leighton stepped over the wrestling pair and crouched down by the base of the newly erected pole. After several seconds of examining the support brace they built to keep the sixteen gauge four and a half inch diameter pole from tilting, or lilting as Bray called it, he looked up at Bray. "I think we're good. The pole is still level and we've got another ten minutes or so."

Finley shook his head in amazement. Before Danielle's arrival, Leighton wouldn't have joined the others with the project, much less gone through the motions of easing Bray's unnecessary concerns. Before the cement completely dried, Finley beckoned Foster over with a wave of his hand. Uncle Finley had a promise to keep.

Jackson lifted his hands from Foster's head as the pup struggled free of his father's grasp. "Ready?"

"Yep. Ready. But remember, it's permanent."

The pup ran up the porch and stormed into the Lodge at a full-tilt run.

"What did you tell my kid he could do, Fin?" Jackson delivered a perfect imitation of Eleanor's side eye.

Finley shrugged. Not living in a single place for more than three months before he turned fifteen, made Finley appreciate the idea of permanence. A lot of people took it for granted and didn't understand how demoralizing it was to move from place to place with all your things stuffed in a black garbage bag. His last foster parents had been different and his foster dad still reached out, just to touch base, but their house still wasn't Finley's home. It wasn't until he arrived at Bray's front door, snatched from boot camp and dragged to Broken Peak, when Finley began to understand that the place where you slept and lived didn't have to be temporary.

Even though Foster was loved by everyone in the pack and his home was Broken Peak as much as it was for the rest of the Pack, it wouldn't hurt to let the pup leave a bit of himself at the Lodge. That way, no matter what happened or where he went, there would always be a part of him here at Broken Peak.

Speak of the devil.

Foster barreled out the front door and left it wide open. Not that he could close it, though. His arms overflowed with all the ephemera he'd accumulated since Eleanor and Foster arrived just a few months ago.

Wait? Was that Hampstead in his rollerball?

Before the clear plastic received a coating of quick-dry cement and the furball had an entirely new type of prison he'd need to break out of, Finley snatched the ball from the pile and saved Hampstead.

"What are you doing with all your things, Foster?" Eleanor stepped on to the front porch, along with Danielle, Maggie, and Vixen.

"Unca Finley said I could."

"First, you didn't answer my question. And second, Uncle Finley says you can do a lot of things, not all of them are good ideas."

"You know he's four, right? I'm not sure logic and reason are skills in his tool set, yet." Danielle snorted. "It's not like any males in this group have an abundance of either."

Eleanor rolled her eyes. "Foster?"

The pup squatted at the base of the pole and carefully pressed some of his toy cars into the cement. "In a minute, Mommy."

Leighton and the others stepped closer to the cement and crouched down to examine Foster's arrangement of toys.

"There." Foster stood and brushed his dirty hands off on his jeans, the same brand and exact style as Jackson's jeans. "Now, Vivi will always have me here. When I get old and leave, she can always come out and see a piece of me."

The four females on the porch visibly wilted under Foster's words.

Vixen, the stoic female who cracked occasional smiles, but rarely showed a hint of emotion that wasn't carefully regulated, looked away and brushed the back of her hand across her cheek.

Bray linked his fingers together behind his neck and stared across the short distance at his mate. "Well, you did it, Finley. I didn't think it was possible, but you broke my mate."

"I didn't, Foster did."

"He broke all of them." Allard pushed up from the ground and came to stand by Finley. He pushed his shoulder against Finley's and shoved his hands deep in his pockets. "You're the mastermind behind it. You did good."

Finley looked away from the females on the porch and turned his attention to the males of his pack. Without a word to each other, Jackson, Leighton, and Tevin raced across the lawn to the Lodge, where they shoved each other out of the way to be the first one inside.

Allard followed right behind them, but stopped and looked back at Finley. "What are you waiting for? An invitation?"

Finley shook his head and ducked his chin to his chest.

"If you don't do it, I'm going to pick something and you probably won't like it. At all." Allard threatened.

"Yeah fine." Finley didn't feel entirely comfortable leaving a piece of himself locked away in cement. Despite Broken Peak being the closest thing to his home, it wasn't home. Not really. Not the same way his own pack territory would be.

"It's not for you, Fin. It's for her." Bray lifted his chin toward Vixen with a slight grin. "Do it for her. You're hers. Doesn't matter what happens years from now, you'll always be hers."

Before Danielle or Eleanor added to Finley's guilt, he shrugged and headed for the front door. As he passed Maggie, he recognized the far-off look on her face. Her raccoon was pushing toward the surface. Both female and animal were considering something, and it wouldn't be the last time Finley wished he had a glimpse inside the workings of her mind.

"What do you wanna bet Jackson picks a pair of Eleanor's panties?" Allard asked as he waited for Finley to catch up.

"The usual. She'll put a stop to it before he steps foot out of their room with them in hand."

CHAPTER FOURTEEN

"**YOUR** girlfriend is strange."

"She's not my girlfriend."

"Okay, your female friend."

"Shut up." Finley reached his arm out to the side and pressed his palm against Allard's face. Not enough to cause his friend's wolf to push for a fight, but enough to convey his frustration with the current topic of conversation.

"He's not wrong."

"You too, Bray?"

"What? No, not about the girlfriend, but by your reaction to her and response to those three males in town, she is. I meant that she's odd."

Long after every member of the pack pushed an item into the almost dry cement, Maggie began climbing the pole that was to hold the massive bird feeders Vixen ordered. Well, not Maggie, Maggie's raccoon. For the past hour and a half, the raccoon shimmied up the pole to the crossbars, then slid back to the ground, where she promptly climbed back up again.

The three males had been standing on the porch and watching the raccoon's antics for the past hour. The sight of the raccoon doing what amounted to a pole dance shouldn't have entertained them as much as it did, but none of them had budged since discovering her.

"You should probably stop calling her Pocket and start calling her Itsy Bitsy." Allard snickered.

"One, why Itsy Bitsy? And B, how do you know I call her Pocket?"

"She's like the spider who crawls up the waterspout only to get washed out and has to climb back up again." Allard's shoulders shook with laughter at what he apparently thought was an amusing observation. Finley wasn't so sure. "And you call her Pocket all the time. I doubt you even realize it."

"You do. At lunch you asked, and I quote, Pocket, what do you want on your sandwich?" Bray agreed. "I got to have this chat with Jackson, but missed out on Leighton. It's gonna hit you hard when you realize it, and you'll do your best to ignore it and pretend it's not happening. You'll have an urge to get drunk, I know I did, don't fight it. Get shit faced, attempt to convince whoever's listening that it's not happening, then in the morning, when you're sober and hungover, embrace that it's happening."

"What the hell are you talking about?" Finley glowered at Bray. Sure, he had an idea that Bray was talking about Maggie being his mate, but as long as he didn't acknowledge it, it wasn't happening. And Maggie had made it clear that it wasn't happening with her insistence on leaving pack territory.

"I didn't think it was possible. Finding that female who fits together with you so perfectly, you can't imagine what life was like before them. But Vi is the best thing that happened to me and this pack."

"She's your lobster."

"What?" Both Finley and Bray spoke at the same time and stared at Allard. Allard said strange things now and again, but this was by far the weirdest.

"Danielle has been marathoning *Friends*." Allard spoke as though his words explained everything. And they probably did in another reality somewhere, but it wasn't one where Bray and Finley were present.

The hinges of the front door creaked as it opened and Bray glanced over his shoulder. "We need to WD-40 those."

"What are you doing out here?" Vixen closed the door and stepped next to Bray.

"Watching Maggie, Pocket, or Itsy Bitsy, depending on who you ask." Bray wrapped his arm around Vixen's shoulder and pulled her against his side.

"What?"

"Never-mind."

"Maggie's been climbing up and down that pole for over an hour." Allard explained Maggie's actions, but conveniently left out how the males knew she'd been climbing for an hour.

Vixen studied the scene in front of her, the repetitive slow methodical climb to the top and the quick slide back to the bottom. On the fifth slide, Vixen smiled. One of her wide grins that bared her teeth and couldn't hide any of her enthusiasm.

"What are you grinning about?" Bray eyed Vixen's smile with a mild amount of concern. Her grins usually accompanied a plan that didn't always bode well for the males. They all remembered the group costume Vixen convinced them to wear.

"That's a powder coated pole with an anti-traction coating. How is it possible a raccoon shifter, who's heavier than her animal counterpart, can get more traction than them?" Vixen wasn't asking for an answer. It was more of her voicing her thoughts. Similar to her big smiles, speaking her thoughts aloud usually meant she was concocting a plan.

With a pat on Bray's chest, she slipped out from under his arm and headed across the lawn. She avoided Maggie on the pole and instead walked to the edge of the woods. Hands on hips, she stared out into the forest for several minutes, before turning back around and heading inside the Lodge. All without a single word to anyone.

"What do you think she's up to?" Finley mused.

"No fucking clue," Bray answered.

The males shrugged off Vixen's brief interruption and resumed observing Maggie's pole exercise. It really shouldn't have been as entertaining to them as it was. Leighton joined them a few minutes later. Whether he was looking for them, specifically Finley, or accidentally stumbled on them, Leighton didn't share. He was suddenly there and part of the conversation.

Bray scratched his fingernails across the whiskers on his cheeks. "I think it's about time you shared everything you know, Leighton."

"About what?"

"Gazes." Bray crossed his arms over his chest and stared out at Maggie with narrowed eyes. "Considering what they did to her camper, it will help to know what we can expect. If anything at all."

Finley wanted to shout that it wasn't Leighton's story to tell, that Maggie should be the one to tell it, but he understood Bray's predicament. Even if he didn't agree with the approach.

Leighton turned his back to the yard and leaned against the porch railing. "I don't know much."

"You know more than the rest of us." Bray pulled his stare away from Maggie and turned it toward Leighton. "Even if she told us everything, it would be tainted by her view. You and Mac are probably the best ones to give us the information we need and Mac's not here."

"He's probably keeping his distance after he met with Maggie. She might not have said it outright, but I don't think she likes Mac all that much." Finley said the closest thing in support of Bray's demand of Leighton, but neither he nor his wolf were happy about it.

"I didn't think it was possible to be angry with Mac, what could he have possibly said that pissed her off?"

"No idea, but as soon as she left his cabin she wanted out of here. Demanded to go back to the camper." Finley filled in the missing bits he knew about, but it wasn't a good answer.

"He showed her the journal entry Eleanor found." Bray supplied the rest.

"Shit. No wonder she got the hell out of Dodge." Allard rubbed the side of his face with his knuckles. "I couldn't figure out why Vixen avoided the subject of Maggie sticking around."

"Wait? You think Maggie wants to leave here because of something Mac said?" Finley snapped at Allard. Not that his friend deserved his anger, but his wolf was close to reaching his frustration limit.

Allard shrugged, "it wouldn't surprise me. Mac's convinced the entry is like a prophecy, and both Vixen and Eleanor are buying into his idea."

"Danielle thinks it's no different from the horoscopes in newspapers and magazines, easy to fit your life into its shape because you want it to. I haven't paid any attention to it."

Everyone except Bray looked at Allard for more information. "It's nothing specific, just that Vixen's appearance, well not Vixen, but her animal, is the sign of big changes for the shifters and she'll surround herself with others described in the journal. I'm guessing Mac thinks Maggie is the Rebel, but it's a generic enough description and she fits it because she's a raccoon shifter."

Bray sighed and sat down on the swing. "All fine and good, but this isn't answering any of my questions about Gazes."

Leighton appropriated Bray's previous pose and crossed his arms over his chest. "It's a long story, you're going to want to sit down for this."

Allard sat down next to Bray on the swing, but Finley didn't budge. Something in the way Leighton spoke set Finley's wolf on edge. Even more than he had been, which was saying a lot since his wolf had been anxious ever since they found Maggie's camper destroyed and her possessions strewn about. He planted his feet and crossed his arms over his chest, mirroring Leighton's stance without the air of relaxation.

"There are good packs and bad packs. Good prides and bad prides. Good clans and bad clans."

"Yeah, yeah, your point?" Bray circled his hand in front of him with an impatience he hadn't shown since Vixen's arrival.

"There are no good Gazes."

"None?" Allard didn't bother hiding his incredulity at Leighton's claim.

"None. They're all tied together under one leader. Or at least they used to be before he died and only left daughters. Now, all the leaders are supposed to be equal, but the wealth of the Gaze determines their ranks." Leighton stuck his leg out and planted his heel in a crack between the boards that made up the porch. "And the leaders will do whatever they deem necessary to gain more wealth. I haven't heard of them hiring out their enforcers as contract killers, but it wouldn't surprise me, assuming the price was right.

"They'll pimp out the females as soon as they come of age, but again, for the right price, I don't think age is a concern."

Finley's claws poked through and dug into his sides, biting the flesh and muscles protecting his ribs, at the thought of Maggie, his Pocket, being pimped out to the highest bidder. "Are you say–"

"No." Leighton cut his hand through the air. "I mean, I can't say for sure, but I don't think so. I've seen those females before and they've all been drugged up. Maggie's dad probably kept her safe and away from the leader's attention. And he probably did it at a considerable cost, and it's likely why Maggie wants to get her father out of there as quickly as possible. I don't know anything about her leader, but from my experience, they have no problem eliminating any dissenting voices and they don't bother with hiding the bodies.

"The leaders deal in drugs and arms, begging and stealing, and prostitution. All to keep their power among the leaders. From what little Maggie's said, her leader is no different."

"What does that mean for us?"

Leighton shrugged, "no clue. Gazes are insular and don't mix with other shifters. But then I haven't heard about a pack interfering in Gaze business. The few times I heard about anyone getting involved have been loners with strong ties to human organizations."

"They're worried about exposing shifters to humans?" Allard asked.

"The leaders might all be sociopaths and ego maniacs, but even with all their guns, they can't go against the entire shifter population and expect to win."

"What does that mean for us? Do you think they'll trespass into our territory?" Bray didn't care about the politics of Gazes, he just cared what it meant for the pack.

Every day with Bray was a new learning experience for Finley. He didn't particularly agree with Bray's choice to ignore what was an apparent wrong in the shifter world, but understood the Pack always had to come first. The realization might have said something about Finley's maturity level, or it might have signified that he was closer to being ready to lead his own pack. In the long run, it didn't matter. What mattered to Finley was the here and now in front of him, and that was all about Maggie's well-being and safety.

"They dole out punishments to insiders for outsiders' transgressions. I doubt they'll come after us, but they will go after Maggie's dad."

"So we get him out of there. As soon as Danielle says it's safe, we go in and extract him. What's the point of having a Vixen if no one knows about her?"

Bray leveled his stare at Finley, and he shrank back from the powerful gaze. Damn, he needed to learn how to do that. Bray's stare was up there with Eleanor's counting trick.

"What do you think will happen when word gets out across all shifters? Right now only a few packs know and they're nervous as fuck. No one wants to give up power once they have it. Hell, the reason why humans revere their first president is because the man willingly gave up power when they all knew damn well they wouldn't do the same in his position. The Alphas don't like the idea of a central power, which is apparently what Mac is convinced Vixen is supposed to be. It's bad enough she's a female, but that she can–"

"Rip their spines out." Jackson filled in with a slight grin on his mouth. Vixen's griffin eviscerated the humans who came for her the night her animal woke when Bray claimed her. Later they learned the female could be just as vicious with her hands as with her beak and talons.

"That too, but there's more to her than her griffin. Revealing that to a Gaze will cause us to fight multiple wars. Let's worry about the humans first before we start shaking up the shifters." Bray's words had the finality of an official decree.

Something the Alpha rarely did.

CHAPTER FIFTEEN

WHAT'S *Batman's guilty pleasure?* Maggie studied the cards in her hand. None of them would make anyone sitting at the table laugh, but if she used a throwaway, it might be perfect for another hand.

This sucked.

When Maggie first heard about game night, she imagined something like sitting around a bonfire and drinking every time someone said a word.

Or a shifter version of capture the flag. Or horseshoes. Hell, even a few games of corn hole would be preferable to sitting around a table and playing cards with words on them you thought someone else would pick. At least with the other games, the mated pairs didn't have such an advantage. Except for Bray and Vixen, but Maggie figured that had more to do with Vixen and less to do with the strength of their bond.

She narrowed down her choices to *mouth herpes* and *construction worker fantasies*. Without looking, she threw a card down on the table. It was only after looking down at her hand and seeing the *construction worker fantasies* card that she fully realized the stupidity of her throwing whatever card down tactic. She shrunk down in her chair as Bray read off the different phrases on the cards the others played.

"Any news on the IDs?" Maggie gave up any pretense of playing the card game and turned away to look at Danielle. The one responsible for the evening of board games.

"We placed the order and Vixen has someone in place to pick them up and deliver them. Since she can't pick them up herself, it will take a few more days before we get all the documents." Danielle stared at the cards on the table, as if she was willing Bray to choose hers. "This isn't just a driver's license, Vixen has birth certificates, social security cards, and an entire history being made for you and your dad. Give it a few more days."

"You know, all of these choices are bad, right?" Bray asked no one as his hand hovered over a card.

Danielle held her breath and Bray shifted his hand to the card next to it.

Something about being crushed to death by vending machines. No doubt Vixen's card.

When he picked it up, Danielle groaned out her defeat loud enough for all the shifters to lift their shoulders to their ears. "Oh, come on, there is not a single reality where Batman would enjoy crushing people with vending machines."

"You don't know that." Vixen snatched the card and placed it on top of the only other winning card she had.

Unfortunately for Danielle, she held her breath whenever anyone got close to picking her card, and apparently Maggie wasn't the only one who would rather play anything else. Only Leighton consistently picked Danielle's cards, but that was because they were freshly mated and their bond was still forming. Leighton wasn't going to do anything to piss his new mate off. Frankly, after spending her time with the pack, she got it. The mates here weren't anything like the mates in the gaze.

Finley looked across the table and winked at Maggie.

When they first sat down, she wondered why he didn't sit next to her, but instead let Danielle and Eleanor take the seats on either side. She tried to hide her disappointment at the time. Partially because she didn't want the others to notice, but a bigger part was she didn't want to consider what that disappointment meant in the scheme of things.

It was bad enough having her animal singing the mine song on repeat. But that was all before the game got started. Once the cards were dealt, Finley spent as much time staring at her as looking at his cards. His foot pressed against hers and when it was her turn to read a card, he always drew it for her and made sure his hand brushed hers during the hand-off. She blushed and looked away before anyone could see the flush race up her cheeks from her neck.

Vixen eyed the few cards in front of her. The female had a competitive streak a mile wide and did not enjoy not winning one bit. "Okay, last hand."

Bray snorted, but instead of asking why Vixen decided the game was over, he drew a card and passed it to Finley to read aloud, like the wise male he was.

"I've got rhythm. I've got music. I've got blank. Who could ask for anything more?"

Maggie didn't bother looking at her other cards. She placed *construction worker fantasies* on the table face down and leaned back in her chair.

Her father would have liked this game.

She thought about him a lot lately. Vixen swore she had someone watching him, ready to pull him out if Zachery tried anything. Mac explained to Vixen that if the bond with her mother wasn't severed before leaving the Gaze, her dad wouldn't survive the extraction, and Vixen agreed there wasn't any point in pulling him out until they got all the documents from the forger.

Maggie limited herself to asking Danielle about the IDs once a day and had already used the day's ration. Thoughts of her dad blocked out what was happening around her until Eleanor choked on her drink in a bout of laughter. Jackson patted her back, but was laughing just as hard.

When she looked up, Finley was staring across at her with a hunger in his bright turquoise eyes. Crapsicles. What did she miss?

Vixen wasn't any help. She had buried her face against Bray's chest and her shoulders shook with barely contained laughter.

"Well, I guess we know who won that round." Danielle grinned at everyone like a deranged squirrel.

"What?" Maggie looked at all the grinning idiots sitting around her, except for Finley, he wasn't grinning like an idiot, he was grinning like a male about to plunge into a seven course gourmet dinner and Maggie was the main course. She swallowed hard and willed her raccoon to stop hopping around screaming mine over and over. "What did I miss?"

"Hold on." Danielle held up a finger while jumping up from the table and running from the room. "Don't go anywhere. I'll be right back."

Maggie lowered her brows and glowered at Allard, who had remained remarkably quiet all evening, but was currently nodding slowly with a knowing grin. Like the answer to the meaning of life had been revealed to him. "What?"

"It's better seen than heard."

"Speak for yourself." Jackson grumbled and a low growl rolled from his chest.

Finley broke his stare and snapped his head toward Jackson at the sound of the growl. His shoulders pushed back and his chest thrust forward, taking up most of the space in the already large kitchen. Finley's wolf pressed close to the surface if the fresh claw marks on the wooden tabletop were anything to go by.

"Boys." Vixen interrupted the fight before it broke out.

Both males deflated slightly, but Jackson's low rumbling growl remained.

Maggie watched it all with wide eyes and, if she was being completely honest with herself, a growing sense of excitement. She'd seen the wolves in the woods, but they liked to keep their distance from her. Witnessing two dominant wolves, males who could easily be Alphas of their own packs, fight would have been a lot more entertaining than an evening of board games.

Tevin cackled from his perch at the head of the table across from Vixen and Bray. Maggie had the sense the others gave him that particular place of honor, not because he was stronger than them, but it wasn't worth the hassle to make him move. Plenty of males in the Gaze were the same, taking and getting liberties because it was easier than fighting them. Except Maggie hadn't witnessed any sadism in Tevin that accompanied the raccoon males.

"You ruined her fun, Vixen. I think she's pouting."

Whatever posturing Finley did with Jackson was child's play compared to his response to Tevin. His canines elongated and punched down over his bottom lip. The bright turquoise eyes didn't just glow, they swirled with a golden light. And those claws that scratched the table? They now dug into the hard wood.

Maggie was surprised Finley wasn't a wolf right then. She'd never seen partial shifts like this before. Either a shifter was an animal or not, nothing in between. "Holy–"

"Boys." Vixen's reprimand cut through the growing heaviness, thick in the air.

Every shifter in the room jerked back as though Vixen pulled them away from one another by the backs of their collars. Except she was still sitting in her chair.

"What the–" Danielle skidded back into the kitchen with a large picture in a frame in her hands. She took one look around the room and shook off the sight as if it was an everyday occurrence. "Vixen your Alpha awesomeness is leaking again."

Maggie closed her eyes and took a breath. The weight in the room had lifted as soon as Danielle said something to Vixen, but holy hell, that was some powerful shit and Maggie needed a minute. When she opened her eyes, everyone in the room was back to normal. The laughter and teasing resumed as if Finley's wolf hadn't challenged not one, but two other wolves.

Eleanor leaned over and whispered, "don't worry, nothing bad will happen, this happens often enough. Put six dominant wolves in a house and there's bound to be some wrestling. No one gets hurt too bad and Vixen is good at stopping it before it gets out of hand."

Danielle plopped down in her chair and shoved the picture into Maggie's hand. "Here. Look at this. And you totally won the game, by the way. Which isn't fair at all, but I'll survive."

Maggie looked down at the picture and laughed. It sounded a little crazy to her ears, but only a little. The picture showed all the males of the pack dressed in sexy versions of costumes. There was a cop, a biker, a sailor, a cowboy, a Native American, and right in the middle of the line-up was Finley dressed in a construction worker's costume, complete with a screwdriver held between his teeth. "When was this?"

"Halloween." Eleanor dragged her fingertip along the glass covering the photo. "We wanted to make Foster's Halloween special, so Vixen ordered the costumes and we trick-or-treated at Mac's and Roose's."

"Oh, you haven't met Roose yet. We need to fix that." Danielle looked around Maggie at Eleanor and grinned wildly, as though her mind had concocted a brilliant plan. "We didn't have a big Thanksgiving because every meal has enough food to qualify as Thanksgiving and there aren't any TVs to park ourselves in front of and watch football as we pass out from food comas. But maybe you'll be around for Christmas."

Maggie calculated the days to Christmas, a holiday no one at the Gaze celebrated, but had no problem marketing to the tourists who visited the gift shop. Almost three weeks away. Hopefully Vixen's friend will have delivered the IDs by then and Maggie and her Dad would be starting their new life far away from the east coast.

The weight of Finley's stare was too powerful to ignore, and she glanced up, daring to look into his mesmerizing turquoise gaze. Damn, that color was compelling. Inviting her to stick around just so she could see it every day for the rest of her life.

Wait? What?

Where the hell had that thought come from?

Mine. Mine. Mine. Mine.

Ah, her raccoon. Of course, the furry beast would do whatever she could to get what she wanted.

"Mmm." Instead of repeating her raccoon's thoughts, Maggie went with the good ol' standby of the sound of non-committal. If the sound was an actual word, it would be somewhere between maybe and perhaps. Closer to *yes* than *no*, but not yet to *we'll see*, which almost always meant yes, on the commitment scale.

CHAPTER SIXTEEN

FINLEY leaned into the kitchen and looked around. Eleanor sat at the table with Foster, working on his sight words, but no one else was in the room. He thought for sure Pocket would be there. After looking almost everywhere else, Finley figured out Maggie was still inside the Lodge, but she wasn't in any of her usual haunts. "Have you seen, Pocket?"

Eleanor slid a flashcard in front of Foster, who crossed his little arms over his chest and scowled at the letters. Finley had spent some time going over sight words with the pup and didn't blame Foster. The flashcards sat squarely on the side of evil as far as Finley was concerned.

While Foster studied the letters, Eleanor lifted her head and smiled at Finley. The smile wasn't one of those polite smiles, it was the conniving smile that always accompanied an idea Eleanor considered great and most of the pack considered not-great. Like dressing up as the Village People for Halloween.

"I think I saw her with Danielle." Eleanor paused and took a deep breath, but Finley high-tailed it out of there before she could vocalize the rest of her thoughts.

"Thanks!" He called out as he headed towards Danielle's computer room.

Of all the sights Finley expected to find when he stopped in front of the open door of Danielle's office, the one that greeted him wasn't anywhere on the list. Or on anyone's list.

Danielle sat in front of her bank of computers in one of the expensive, but totally comfortable chairs that Finley had considered stealing and bringing to his room on more than one occasion, typing furiously away on the keyboard.

Next to her, in a matching chair, a raccoon sat similarly, with her paws slamming away at another keyboard. Pocket didn't usually let her animal out inside. The beast liked to steal things, which was fine, as long as they found her latest hiding spot. But she'd gotten better at hiding things and it had taken them over three hours to find Hampstead happily rolling around in his hamster ball in the underground tunnels, because why wouldn't a raccoon think the underground tunnels were a perfect place to hide things?

Finley leaned against the doorjamb with his ankles crossed and his hands in his pockets. Normally, he'd have chastised Danielle. Their guest wasn't entertainment, but watching the two females, one hard at work, the other copying the first because the raccoon loved to touch things almost as much as she enjoyed stealing things, hinted at a future Finley hoped for, but accepted wouldn't be likely because of Maggie's insistence she couldn't stay at Broken Peak.

Seconds, or maybe several minutes passed before Danielle paused her typing to study the lines on the screen. The raccoon stopped typing as well. At first he didn't understand why. Usually when Pocket's hands were busy doing something, they didn't stop their task until someone pulled the object away.

Danielle sighed and reached into a small container on the desk, pulled out a grape, and handed it to Pocket.

Ah. That would be why.

If it was possible for Maggie's raccoon to have an Achilles heel, it was grapes. From the way she went bonkers for Oreos, you'd have thought cookies were the way to her heart, but nope. Grapes were the secret to getting whatever you wanted her raccoon to give up.

"I don't get it, Maggie. The system worked for you, but it hasn't pulled anything else out. The feed is still active, but my code isn't finding anything."

Finley heard Danielle's words, but didn't understand them. Whatever she did at her computers was well above his pay grade. Hell her computer skills were well above the rest of the Pack's pay grade. But both he and his wolf enjoyed seeing Danielle talk to Maggie's raccoon as though the female understood Danielle and could respond.

Another sigh and another grape.

Finley could have watched them all day. And he would have, except General Jesup made one of his impromptu visits.

"What's going– " The older man stepped next to Finley and leaned into the room. It didn't take more than a second before spotting Maggie's raccoon sitting next to Danielle. "Oh."

"Argh!" Danielle squealed out a scream of shock at the noise and spun around her chair to face the door with her hand covering her heart. "Sheesh, you scared me. How long have you been here?"

The raccoon stood up on her hind legs and peered over the back of her chair before Danielle reached over and spun the second chair around for the raccoon.

Finley grinned at the gesture. He liked that the other females accepted his female so easily. Yes, he knew calling her his was premature. But she was. She'd say she wasn't until she fell over, but neither Finley nor his wolf bought her protests.

"Not long," Finley lied.

The General chuffed, but didn't comment further on the subject. "Ms. Howe, I have an assignment for you."

"Come on, Pocket, you can spend some time with me." The raccoon stared at him with the impassive confidence of a queen on her throne and waved her paw toward the woman next to her. Before Finley got pulled into said assignment, he stepped into the cluttered space, scooped Maggie off the chair, and grabbed the container of grapes. "If you keep giving her raccoon these, we won't be able to use them as bribery anymore."

The raccoon leaned out of her cradle in the crook of Finley's elbow and reached for the container, but he held it out of reach as he left Danielle and the General to their assignment discussion. Undaunted, Maggie twisted around and crawled over his shoulders to the other arm and the grapes with a single-mindedness that bordered too close to her wild counterpart for Finley's comfort.

"Come on, Pocket, it's time to let Maggie out." For whatever odd reason, the raccoon responded to Finley's nickname for Maggie, more so than she responded to Maggie's name.

The raccoon chittered back her distaste for Finley's suggestion.

"Yeah, Pocket, I get it, but there will be more grapes for you later, I promise." Finley moved the container to his other hand, thwarting the raccoon from reaching her goal and earning him another round of chittering.

"Pocket, please?"

The raccoon stared at him as though he was the stupidest male she'd ever encountered, thinking he could convince her to shift back with the promise of grapes in the future. He detoured to the kitchen, dropped the grapes off on the counter while wrangling Pocket away from her treat.

"You found her." Eleanor announced.

"You didn't tell me she shifted." Finley admonished Eleanor. He hadn't fully appreciated the struggles of raising a rambunctious pup until he spent time with Maggie's raccoon. Some days it was like living with a toddler who had ten little razors and the will and determination to destroy everything in her path.

"You can call it karma, Uncle Finley." Eleanor pulled Foster back into his seat and tapped the paper sitting on the table in front of him. "Three more sums and you can have wolf time with your dad."

Apparently raccoon shifters and four-year-old boys were more similar than Finley thought possible if both could be easily bribed with simple treats. With Maggie once again safely tucked in the crook of Finley's elbow, he waved goodbye to Eleanor and Foster then headed out the kitchen and down the hallway to his bedroom. Just before he walked into his room, he thought better of it and u-turned.

Pocket didn't need any more time in his room to steal things. The raccoon had absconded with the few personal items of his and had started to take a liking to his electronic gadgets, the ones Danielle gave to the team. After three nights of hearing a raccoon chittering into a neck mike that broadcasted to the earpieces worn by those on patrol, Vixen delivered a small lockable safe to keep Maggie's raccoon away from the more sensitive gadgets.

Instead, he headed to her bedroom. Plus, Maggie might be able to push her raccoon back inside if she had the security of her room. He tossed the raccoon onto the bed, something she apparently enjoyed because she had wrangled Finley into playing the game for an hour just the day before, and closed the door before she could escape and make a dash back to the kitchen and what she likely considered her grapes.

The raccoon turned her face away from him and chittered. It hadn't taken long for Finley to decipher the raccoon's noises. Really, there were only two. Happy and pissed. The sound coming from her right then was definitely pissed.

"Pocket..."

The raccoon turned her back to Finley and sat down on the bed.

"Come on, shift back. I want to talk with Maggie, but I can't do that with you out."

The raccoon ignored him. The equivalent of a toddler holding her breath before a full-blown temper tantrum started.

"You can run with the pack if you let Maggie out, but you have to let her out now."

He didn't know if what he said got through to Maggie or the raccoon, but one moment he was looking at the furry back of a raccoon and the next his eyes settled on the smooth curve of a female's bare back.

His cock punched against his fly, announcing its presence. Try as he might, shifting his weight from leg to leg didn't help matters, and he had to rely on his hand to make things more comfortable.

"I think there's a clean shirt in the top drawer of the dresser." Maggie's voice was rough and from the slow undulations of her body as she stretched her arms and legs, her muscles were just as sore.

"How much time are you giving your raccoon, Pocket."

She glanced over her shoulder and a glimpse of her pink nipple peaked out at him, mocking his current dilemma. Act on the urge to get between her legs or have the grown up conversation about giving her animal too much time?

Finley snapped his eyelids closed and stumbled his way to the dresser. He didn't open his eyes until he faced the dresser, but hadn't considered the mirror hanging on the wall.

Fuck.

He could so do this. Right? Keep eyes closed, open the drawer, and grab the first thing that felt like a shirt, then throw it over his shoulder.

His cock disagreed, but not all the blood had left his brain and he managed those simple tasks in quick succession.

CHAPTER SEVENTEEN

THE soft cotton of the oversized tee shirt brushed down over her bare skin before landing in a small pile in her lap. Maggie shifted around, covering all her bits with the shirt before turning to face Finley's back and his reflection in the mirror.

With his eyes squeezed tightly closed and his lips drawn into a firm thin line, he looked in pain and Maggie fought back the laugh bubbling up.

"When I first came to your territory, I spent more time as a raccoon. She's struggling with losing that freedom after a week of running wild in the woods."

Finley opened one eye and peered at her in the mirror, then opened the other and spun to face her. He crossed his arms over his chest and leaned back against the dresser. "Does she always resist changing?"

The answer wasn't a simple yes or no. A lifetime with the Gaze contributed to Maggie keeping her raccoon hidden away except for the mandatory Gaze events. Her raccoon was small compared to the others. While capable of fighting back with a vengeance, she wouldn't have been able to prevent anyone from taking what they wanted, regardless of her wishes. So, Maggie kept her locked away unless her dad was around to protect her. For the first time in over twenty years, her raccoon was safe, all things considered, and loved the freedom to explore the world around her. Maggie had trouble not giving into her raccoon now, because her raccoon had always been patient and understanding when it mattered most.

"Maggie? Is this new?"

"She's used to me keeping tighter control of her. Plus, it makes Danielle happy to see her."

"Danielle isn't going to get the IDs here any sooner just because she likes your raccoon."

Maggie lifted a shoulder and looked down at the hem of her tee shirt. Leave it to Finley to call her out. Would have been safer just to say yep and leave it at that. Except then Finley would want to fix her. The mattress sank under Finley's weight as he settled on the bed next to her and her body tilted toward him, closing the space between them.

"Why is she used to tighter control, Pocket?"

"Gazes aren't the safest places for females. And she's smaller than normal."

"Pocket?" Finley whispered, then waited for her to look up at him.

She knew what would happen. She'd look in his gorgeous eyes that captivated both her and her raccoon and spill everything. How she dressed in baggier clothes, did everything to appear as unattractive as possible, and avoided any situation where she'd be alone with a male. How she was still a virgin. Granted, it wasn't like she was a forty-year-old virgin, but announcing that not only was she a virgin but the first time she kissed another male was with him. In this room and on this bed less than a week ago, topped the all-time mood killer list.

His fingers tugged at the ends of her hair as he combed through the curls, and she caved and looked at him.

"Dad did his best. To do that, I had to stay away from males. Any males, except for Dad."

"All males?" Finley's eyebrows came together in the middle of his forehead, just above his nose as the meaning of her words hit him.

"All males."

His eyebrows ventured into his hairline. "You don't say."

"Well, yes, I do say, I just said."

Finley shook his head and laughed, then kissed the top of her head. As though she had said something spectacular. She didn't, but then she guessed it was less about what she said and more about the meaning behind what she said. Maggie tilted her head back, wanting him to see the rolling of her eyes. It didn't do any good if he couldn't see the eye rolling.

His mouth captured hers and he kissed her. And not in the hesitant way where she might shatter kiss. His kiss was strong and powerful and made her toes curl. Granted it wasn't the kiss that made her toes curl as much as it was her legs shooting out straight because the muscles in her legs contracted because things got all tingly and her legs going straight stopped her from grinding against Finley like the women who danced on poles in Moundsville. Not that she ever saw them, but a few of the males had sneaked out one night and Maggie overheard them talking about it in the woods the next day.

Finley growled a low and rumbly noise from his chest. The anxiety that had built up from the mere thought of announcing her lack of experience in the bedroom department fell away with a whoosh at the warm sound.

But that was all before Maggie twisted her body into the kiss and moved just enough to climb Finley like a tree, but not do any of the grindy parts and accidentally, okay maybe a little on purpose, sort of brushed the back of her hand across the front of his jeans and ran into an extremely hard dick.

Maggie froze. But didn't move her hand.

Finley froze. But didn't move his lips from hers.

What did Maggie have to lose? Besides her virginity? Had she grown up anywhere else, she'd probably have had sex before landing in her early twenties. And had she met Finley under any other circumstances, they'd already be sharing a bed and probably halfway to a mating if her animal was right, and she usually was with the shifter things.

Now or never.

She opted for now and plunged into the deep end.

The hard muscles of Finley's stomach flexed and twitched under her hand as she dragged her fingers up and under his shirt. Finley wasn't small, but his size didn't showcase his sheer strength and power. Abdominal muscles flexed and coiled, ready to spring into action as soon as his body needed them. But he didn't wear his muscles as a badge of intimidation or a show of strength. He wore them no differently than the old worn jeans and tee shirt that might have been washed one too many times.

The muscles offered a temptation she couldn't ignore, and she pulled her lips away from his mouth. Twisting and turning until she faced him, she leaned forward and lifted his shirt, then kissed each one of the clearly defined muscles. All six of them.

Wait. Nope. Two more. Of course he had an eight pack instead of a six pack. She continued up his chest, lifting his shirt as she went and revealing more of his body. He reached behind his head and pulled his shirt off.

"Why do you do that?"

"Do what?" If Finley was impatient with her question interrupting what they both knew was about to happen, he didn't show it.

"Take your shirt off from the top instead of the bottom." Her eyes never moved from his gloriously bared chest.

"Not sure. Guess it's just easier." Finley reached out and pinched her chin between his thumb and finger. Lifting her face up until she was looking into his eyes, he smiled down at her. "Hey, Pocket, this is all about you. You are deciding everything. You don't have to do anything at all, you know that, right?"

"What? Why? I mean, yeah, but why?"

Finley cracked a smile and waved his hand back and forth between the two of them. "Because in my experience, people don't usually care how the clothes come off when at the clothes taking off portion of events."

Okay, so maybe a few of the nerves lingered in the outskirts, waiting for the right moment to pounce and announce their presence to everyone in the room. What should have been a romantic moment shifted into a full-on awkward teen movie moment.

"Yeah, well, okay." What else was there to say, really?

Finley laughed a soft chuckle and his mouth found her lips. His tongue played and danced with hers.

As far as Maggie was concerned, Finley was a great kisser. Not that she had anyone to compare him too, but if her body's response was anything to go by, he was at the top of his game. His hands cradled her neck and brought her face closer to him and deepened his kiss.

Was that even possible?

What did it matter? She got lost in the kiss and didn't worry about finding herself. Not when love and lust had found her. Alone they were powerful, but together they formed an intoxicating combo that pushed her nerves aside.

When he rolled her on to her back and caged her on the bed with his powerful body, she wasn't nervous or worried about the virginity thing. Without using any words, just a kiss, Finley eased her concerns until the only remaining care was becoming his.

Until she had to leave Broken Peak. But that didn't matter at the moment.

His hips rolled, pressing down between her legs so her thighs cradled him and his hard cock rubbed against her core.

Oh.

Even with his jeans on, she couldn't deny the size of his erection bordered just on the other side of obscene.

Ignoring her growing arousal, which was difficult to do considering she wasn't wearing any pants, she allowed her thoughts to wander off into the realm of random thoughts. Like, was it painful to be that big and hard and still wearing jeans? How about walking? Did Finley adopt a wide-legged waddle to accommodate the mammoth erection between his legs?

It would just be good manners to relieve any of the potential discomfort, right?

Maggie dragged her hands down his sides to the button and zipper and made quick work of divesting Finley of his pants.

Finley smiled into their kiss and laughed softly. "Pocket, we don't have to rush, we have all the time in the world."

Except they didn't. And Finley knew as well as Maggie that their time was limited. Before that thought embedded itself in her mind, Finley left her mouth and kissed his way down her body, over the shirt until he got to the bottom and pushed it up over her breasts.

His tongue flicked across her clit and Maggie's body jump up from the bed. She'd used her finger on her clit before, but it had never felt like that. She wanted, no needed, more and raised her hips up off the bed to get closer to him.

Finley obliged her unspoken request and lowered his mouth further down, spearing into her with his tongue.

Fingers gripped his hair and blanket and whatever else her hands could grab hold of as a wave of pleasure, so intense it pushed into the realm of too much, rolled through her body, starting at her toes and expanding up and out of her hair.

Yep. Even her hair tingled. What was with his tongue? Did Finley have some kind of secret magic?

Finley growled in appreciation, and the pleasure expanding throughout her body reeled back in and focused on her core. Before she understood what was happening, the wave of pleasure exploded, lighting all her nerve endings and pushing into an otherwise unknown and unexperienced realm of complete and unadulterated pleasure.

Maggie's fingers speared into his hair, yanking Finley's head away before her nerve endings exploded in a second wave of uncontrolled pleasure.

She screamed out his name, not caring who or what might hear her.

Finley slid back up her body, his lips finding hers again and his tongue speared into her mouth. The intensity of his kiss might have been enough to push that second wave of pleasure, but her mind was gone to the land of fairies, happily rolling about in the field of pleasure her body erected from all of Finley's wonderful touches.

The male released a satisfied growl and what do you know? Another wave of pleasure slowly built up. While the pleasure built, Finley took control. Not that he hadn't been in control before, but this was different. Maggie didn't worry about anticipating what he wanted from her. Without hesitation, she gave what he demanded.

Her body tingled with pleasure, as though woken up for the first time in her life, with each kiss, nibble, and bite Finley left on her skin.

"Pocket?"

"Yeah." She wasn't sure she had managed to get the word out until his face came into view.

"You ready, baby?"

Maggie nodded.

"Need words, Pocket." The head of his cock pressed against her entrance. "Tell me if you want me to stop, baby."

"Don't stop. Please don't stop."

He kissed down her neck, across her breast, each nipple, then back up her neck to her lips. "I need you, Pocket. Right now."

Maggie had never been needed. Wanted, sure, but not in the same way Finley wanted her. Euphoria at the purity of Finley's needs warred with the pleasure that still hadn't abated.

Finley eased first one, then two fingers into her and pressed his thumb against her clit.

Maggie had a new number one for best days in her life and as far as she understood it, they still hadn't gotten close to finishing. Sure, she'd had an orgasm. A mind-blowing, earth-moving, world-shattering orgasm, and that would have been enough to be at the top of her list, but from the way Finley moved his fingers in her, there was so much more to come.

She giggled at the pun, and Finley's glowing turquoise eyes found hers.

"What's so funny, Pocket?"

"Nothing. Just this is the best day yet." Her voice hitched as his fingers found a particular spot inside of her she had no idea existed.

"Oh, it's about to get a lot better." Finley rolled to his side and watched his fingers move in and out of her before shifting his gaze back to her face and eyes.

Maggie watched him watch her. The way his concentration showed on his face with little crinkles and wrinkles. Or how his messy hair flipped and flopped as he moved his attention along the length of her body. She studied the movement of his muscles, the hunger in his eyes, and the positively mammoth erection jutting proudly out at full attention.

Yeah, the fingers might be great and all, but she wanted the huge thing between his legs, happily seated between her legs and inside of her. Maggie had enough of waiting and hooked her leg around Finley's hip and pulled him back on top of her. Finley removed his hand, which was a bit of a disappointment, and placed it on the bed to keep himself from dropping his weight down on Maggie. Before he protested or insisted on using a word like patience, Maggie reached down and wrapped her hand around the base of his cock, lifted her hips just right, and guided the head of his cock to her entrance, wet from all of Finley's hard work.

Finley groaned and stared into her eyes. He said nothing, but then he didn't need to. The look in his eyes, the soft growl in his chest, and the close presence of his wolf screamed a single word her own beast had been singing on repeat since Maggie shifted back.

Mine.

Finley slid into her slowly, allowing her body to adjust to his girth. He moved in and out in a slow progression until his cock was halfway inside her. Except it felt like he was completely inside. She wiggled her hips and lifted them up, and his cock slid the rest of the way.

She was no longer a virgin.

Okay, the earth didn't do its shaking this time and her world wasn't rocked.

All things considered, it was mildly uncomfortable.

Maybe they should have stuck with the tongue on her clit thing and not branched out into other areas.

Maybe sex wasn't anything like the Grand Canyon and could fail in living up to expectations.

"Pocket, baby, you're so tight."

"Is that bad?" Maybe being tight made things not good, or more difficult to be good.

"No, Pocket, it's not bad at all." Finley laughed and kissed her hard as he slowly moved his hips back and forth, sliding the full length of his cock in and out of her. "But I'm not going to last long, so I need to help you along, because I'll be damned if you don't come one more time."

He reached down between them and pressed his thumb against her clit while sitting back and looking down where they were connected. Maggie watched him staring at his cock moving in and out of her and whether it was his thumb on her clit or the blatant power of his body taking hers or the honest hunger in his eyes that pushed her back close to the edge of an orgasm, she didn't know. Or care.

Finley's fingers pressed into her ass as he grabbed her hip with his free hand and pulled her down hard onto him. Like he could go even deeper.

The tsunami of pleasure slammed into her.

Maggie wasn't expecting it, but it was there, pulling her along on a powerful wave of pleasure that grew and shrunk until it finally pushed her over the edge.

"Mine!" Finley's shout came with a hard thrust as he accompanied her with his own explosion before collapsing over her and kissing her with a ferocity stronger than the fierceness of her orgasm.

She wanted more. She wanted to go again. And not just because her raccoon was surprisingly quiet and content, but because she wanted the best day of her life yet to never end.

Finley tried to roll off her, but Maggie wrapped her arms and legs around his body, so when he rolled to his side, she went with him. He continued on to his back and she sprawled across his chest. Making a huge mess.

"I didn't think sex would be so messy."

He nuzzled her neck and licked at the skin before leaving little bites. Nothing hard enough to leave a mark, but the unspoken intention was clear to both. And Maggie wasn't bothered by it. "It just means we can have more fun in the shower getting clean."

Maggie hummed happily, her fingers playing over the muscles and lines of his chest. More was good. She liked the idea of more.

CHAPTER EIGHTEEN

MAGGIE sat on the edge of Finley's bed and watched as he strapped on layer after layer of gear. Her eyes followed the movement of his hands and fingers as they moved through the practiced routine taken every night before patrol.

"You'll be safe?" Maggie tucked her feet beneath her and tugged at the ends of a lock of hair.

Finley grinned. It was cute the way she worried about him without telling him she worried. He stepped in front of her and lifted his shirt, exposing the black muscle shirt all the Pack wore beneath their clothes while on patrol.

"Feel this."

Her tiny fingers pressed into the fabric then tugged at it, only to have the fabric slip from her fingers and snap back into place. She tilted her head back and looked up at him. "What is it?"

"Body armor. It's good for slowing any weapon down and mitigating any damage. Plus, we have jackets we wear too and our pants even have protection. I'm more safe on patrol than I am wrestling with the boys." Finley pushed her curly hair behind her ear. It acted as a curtain sometimes and hid her face away from him, something he recently learned both he and his wolf did not like one bit. "Vixen and Bray take good care of us, Pocket. They won't let anything happen to us if they can prevent it."

Maggie considered his words before giving him a slow nod. "Okay."

He bent forward and kissed the tip of her nose. "I'll be back soon, I promise, and when I do, we'll have more fun."

It had been all Finley could do to get Maggie out of her bed and to dinner earlier in the evening. But he wasn't complaining.

She grinned and wrinkled her nose at him. "I didn't realize it would be like that or I would have done it much sooner."

"Well, I'm glad you didn't."

"Why?"

"Why? Pocket…" He pinched the bridge of his nose between his thumb and forefinger. How did he explain things without sounding like an asshole? He didn't. "I'll let you figure it out, but I'm sure Eleanor and Danielle can help you."

With a kiss to the top of her head, Finley headed out and joined Allard in the front yard.

"Took you long enough. Thought I'd have to have Tevin take your place." Allard grinned at him. "Or send Vixen in to drag you out of bed."

"I wish." Finley adjusted his erection until it stopped pressing uncomfortably against the zipper of his pants. "But with Pocket, I don't think a quickie is possible. I doubt she even knows the definition of a quickie."

Together they headed towards the woods. They'd worked together so often, they didn't need words to communicate. Their synchronization was one of the reasons Vixen liked to pair them up. She told them it gave her less to worry about, and Bray confessed the worry was whether they'd fight or not. Something the other pairings tended to do.

Less than five minutes into their silent patrol, both their phones vibrated.

"Incursion?"

Finley looked down at his phone screen. "Yep, Northeast. Except..."

"What?" Allard glanced down at Finley's phone. "I'm only see two. Don't they usually send three?"

"Maybe they have a quota and risk going over it."

"That's a budget, not a quota. One's a number you have to reach the other's a number you can't go over."

"Potato, potato."

"No. Not even close." Allard closed his eyes and released a loud breath. "Come on, let's check it out."

The two men barely put up a fight. Either the government was pulling from the bottom of the barrel or it was a suicide mission. Neither option was palatable, though. While Allard dragged the unconscious bodies to a tree where they could bind them until someone could bring them to the shed Vixen used for interrogations, Finley sniffed at the air.

"I don't like it."

"What?" Allard looked up from covering the men's mouths with tape.

"This was too easy." Finley looked down at the unconscious men and their lack of weaponry and equipment. "They know Vixen, right? She probably trained some of the men who trained these men."

"Yeah?" Allard finished off the last steps of binding the two men together. Even if they broke free, they wouldn't get far tied to each other at their ankles and wrists.

"Why come on to her territory barely armed and then not put up a fight when caught?"

"You think they're a distraction?" Allard called in the prisoners' location. Roose or Gareth would come out and bring the men back to the shed while Allard and Finley continued their patrol.

"I know they are." Finley kept his nose in the air, hoping his wolf might help him find something or someone out of place.

"The Lodge is the only place they'd be headed. If they want Foster that badly, they'll have to break in and they know it."

Finley nodded in agreement and both men started back towards the base of the mountain. Halfway back to the Lodge, a scream broke through the silence of the woods. A scream filled with pain and terror. But the sound didn't come from a female or a pup. It came from a man.

"What the…" Finley veered toward the scream and ran faster through the woods with Allard right on his heels.

Pack is nice.

Yeah, I know the pack is nice.

That was the problem, and it would make it difficult for Maggie to leave the pack when the time came. A quick look over her shoulder at the Lodge confirmed no one saw her and followed her outside.

At the wood's edge, she stripped off her clothing and tucked them between a rock and a tree. Not that she was worried anyone would take her clothes, but habits from the gaze died hard.

Mate is strong.

First, not my mate. Second, he might be strong, but it doesn't mean he can't use a little help.

The beast gave her the equivalent of an eye roll and a whatever. Her raccoon had her own idea about how things should be. In fact, she always had, since Maggie was a little girl and didn't have any problems with letting Maggie know her opinions.

Before her raccoon began an abbreviated lecture, Maggie tucked herself inside and let her animal free. It was easier for Maggie to hide inside the animal and ignore the lecture than push the animal aside. Not all shifters had the problem of a strong-willed animal, at least according to Maggie's Dad.

The raccoon scampered up the trunk of a tree and used the branches to move along from tree to tree. She remained far enough away from Finley and Allard, but close enough to keep track of their position by using Finley's scent.

The woods went silent and Maggie froze on the branch. Both she and her raccoon took stock of the situation. Animals didn't go silent unless a predator was around, and even then, it didn't seem likely that the forest animals hadn't gotten used to having the pack around.

The raccoon lifted her snout and wove from side to side.

Anything?

Sniffing.

It was Maggie's turn to deliver an eye roll.

Good woods. Nice to play in.

I get it, okay? You don't have to say anything more.

Wolves are nice.

Yes, I know. You like the wolves.

Flying death monster is nice.

What? What flying death monster?

The scent of a human, one who didn't belong to the pack, stopped Maggie's line of questioning.

Maggie's raccoon hopped from tree branch to tree branch until she found the human male, alone, and much too close to the Lodge for both Maggie and her raccoon's liking. The shadowy figure moved in the direction of the Pack's living quarters, but stayed hidden within the darkness of the woods.

Her raccoon took over, and Maggie didn't fight her. The raccoon leapt from the branch and landed on the invader's head. Claws and fangs dug into the soft flesh of the human's head and didn't relent, even when the invader's hands reached up in an attempt to unsuccessfully pry the raccoon off his face.

"Well, that's not something you see every day." Finley's voice broke through the raccoon's ferocious anger and pushed into Maggie's consciousness, but she didn't pull the raccoon back.

"Is she trying to bite his face off?" Allard cocked his head to the side and studied the scene playing out in front of him.

"Not sure, but if she is, she's succeeding."

"Holy crap, at least she's not Vixen. Can you imagine her in a Vixen?"

Finley sighed, "how are we supposed to separate them?"

"I don't think we do. I think we just wait it out."

"We might be here all night then, because her raccoon doesn't look like she's letting up any time soon."

"I hope Vixen doesn't want to question him. There's no way he'll be able to talk after she's finished with him."

The operative stumbled around the small clearing until he crashed into a tree. The good news was that he knocked himself unconscious. The bad news was that the raccoon took a hit to her head as well.

Finley had never seen a drunk raccoon before, but the way Maggie's animal weebled and wobbled and almost fell down was probably a close approximation. He bent forward and scooped her up, calming the confused raccoon with soothing words of nonsense and soft pets.

"What are we supposed to do with him?" Allard stared down at the unconscious bleeding man who was missing a quarter of his face.

"Slice his throat and call Gareth. We'll have to let Vixen and Bray know one got by us." Finley had no sympathy for the operative. Sure, Maggie could hold her own in a fight and did a damn good job of it, but he tried to hurt her and both Finley and his wolf wanted more blood. He'd do it himself too, if he wasn't worried about the dazed and confused state of the raccoon. Convincing her to let Maggie back was going to be enough of a fight, and he didn't need any of the human's blood on him to rile up the beast even more.

Allard glanced up from his bloody task and lifted his chin toward the dark figure lurking in the shadows just outside the clearing. "I think she already knows."

Vixen stepped out of the trees and greeted both males with a curt nod. She studied the carnage for a moment, looked between Allard and Finley, then settled her gaze on Finley, well, the raccoon in Finley's arms. The little beast received one of Vixen's rare satisfied grins. The type of smile all the males of the pack hoped to receive when she checked in on their training or patrols.

As quickly as she arrived, she disappeared back into the forest.

"Okay, that was freaky." Allard looked back down at the raccoon mauled man.

"Vixen?"

"Yeah."

"You know, sometimes I'm not sure if it's Vixen or her animal. Like the female can be standing there, but it's really her griffin who's doing the observing and commenting."

Allard kicked at the freshly dead body. "I think that's the point. We're separate from our animals, but I don't think she is. And from what Mac and Eleanor have learned, it's supposed to be that way."

"Because she's a griffin? Or are you back on that prophecy kick again?"

"Possibly a little of both. You have to admit it's strange how all the pieces are coming together. Eleanor, Danielle, and now Maggie?"

The raccoon opened her mouth and released a loud chitter.

Finley held Maggie up in front of him and lifted her body so her head was higher than his. Like a parent lifting their toddler in the air. "You're just a fierce little monster, aren't you?"

The raccoon chittered again.

"Yes, you are."

"Now, you're just being weird."

Finley tucked Maggie under his arm, but she wriggled and squirmed, wanting to be set back on the ground. "If I let you down, you need to leave that bad man alone. He's not a chew toy."

The raccoon chittered again, but Finley couldn't tell if she was agreeing or disagreeing.

Allard pulled out his phone and thumbed a quick text while Finley and Maggie's raccoon continued what Allard deemed a weird conversation. He glanced up from the screen and rolled his eyes. "Just put her down and let's get back to the Lodge. Gareth is sending Alex down to take care of the body and the last thing we need is Maggie meeting a mountain lion. Hey, nice alliteration and I wasn't even trying for it."

"What?" Finley looked away from his raccoon's happy, but deranged grin. He heard bits and pieces of what Allard said, but it was difficult not to focus on the raccoon's unabashed glee.

"Nothing. Let's just go." Allard harrumphed, or maybe it was a disgruntled sigh, and shoved into Finley as he passed by him.

Finley shrugged, tucked the raccoon firmly under his arm, and followed. As much as her claws were ultra-sharp razor blades, she did her best not to scratch him. She still struggled to get down, but kept her claws away from his skin.

Sweet raccoon.

CHAPTER NINETEEN

AS FINLEY carried Maggie past the tree where she hid her clothing, she urged her raccoon to redouble her wriggling efforts to escape his grip. Finally, in a last ditch effort, she scrambled up his chest, up over his shoulder, and down his back to the ground.

"Pocket!" Finley spun around and made a half-hearted attempt to catch her, but Maggie made it to the tree with her clothes before Finley could catch her.

Her raccoon skidded to a halt, and Maggie tucked her animal back inside.

"Oh."

Maggie looked over her shoulder and grinned at Finley, standing there shifting his weight from foot to foot. Like he hadn't ever seen her without her clothes on before.

"I'll just…" Finley turned his back to her and growled something low to Allard.

Maggie wasn't paying much attention to him. She was too busy shaking the leaves from her bra and underwear before pulling them on. How was it the leaves found their way into her undies, but stayed clear of her jeans and shirt? Once dressed she headed across the lawn at a jog and caught up with Finley and Allard.

Finley reached back with his arm and waved his hand about. Without a second thought, she reached out and took his hand in hers. A flurry of tingling erupted in her belly and spread a wave of warmth through her body.

He squeezed her hand and tugged her closer to him. "You okay?"

Maggie nodded, "sure."

"You know we're going to have a talk about you going outside while I'm patrolling instead of staying inside." Finley pulled her closer.

"You mean we aren't going to talk about who the scary dude in black was, or that Vixen is a griffin? Because really, those are more important conversations on my list of things we should be talking about." Maggie tightened her fingers around his palm. "Vixen's really a griffin?"

Finley nodded. Not that she expected him to say anything. Words didn't really do justice to a mythical creature coming to life.

"Shower or bath?"

"Nice change of subject."

"Pick one, Pocket."

"I'll give the report to Vixen and have Eleanor drop some food off for Maggie in her room." Allard glanced over his shoulder at them.

"I'm right here, you know. And, hello, no one's answered my question about who the scary dude in black was."

"Adrenaline is still racing through your system. Once it fades, you're going to crash pretty hard." Allard answered her. "We've all been through this before and it's nothing to worry about, but there are ways to make coping easier. That's all we're doing here. Making things easier."

"What are you talking about?" Maggie felt great. Between the tingles caused by Finley's touches and the euphoria from stopping the creepy guy, she wasn't worried.

"Send the food to my room." Finley pulled Maggie through the front door and down the hallway to the wing with the bedrooms. "And let Vixen know I'll talk to her later."

Allard lifted his chin in agreement and separated from Finley and Maggie to find Vixen and whatever else he said he would find.

Finley pushed Maggie into the bathroom and closed the door behind him. "Get undressed."

Her hands moved as if they had a mind of their own and by the time she stripped off her clothes, Finley had the shower running on hot with steam billowing out the top and rolling across the ceiling.

"Get in." Finley offered her his hand and helped her into the shower. "Just stand there for a bit while I grab some towels."

He pulled the curtain closed and a few seconds later the sound of the door opening and closing announced her solitude. She was alone, and that realization hit her full in the chest. Maggie fell back against the cool tiles, using the wall to support her weight before her knees gave up on her and buckled under the exceeding pressure on her chest.

She killed a man. Well, not her exactly. Allard did the deed, but she was the reason Allard killed him.

Kept pack safe.

"Oh shut it."

Maggie banged her head against the tiles and closed her eyes tight. She hadn't talked to her animal out loud since she was little. Her opinionated, independent, and not afraid to make her views known, animal. Once her father realized she talked to her animal with words, he made her stop. The last thing they needed was a reason for Zachery to pay attention to her.

Pack safe. Mate safe.

"Seriously. Just shut it." Maggie pressed the heels of her hands against her closed eyes and slid down the wall until she sat at the floor of the shower with the water pounding down on her.

"The door's closed, Pocket." Finley's voice carried through the sound of the water drops slapping against the curtain and walls.

Shit.

Mine.

Maggie breathed in through her nose and held her breath. It was the trick her father taught her to keep from talking to her animal.

Yeah, fine. I get it. But just...

Maggie didn't need to complete her thought. Her raccoon received the message loud and clear and slipped away from the recesses of her mind.

"Pocket?" The shower curtain rings slid across the metal bar. It took a few seconds for him to look down and find her sitting on the floor of the tub. "Oh, Pocket. I thought I had more time."

She didn't know how much time passed, whether it was minutes or seconds, but one moment her back was against the cool tile and the next it was against his warm chest. His warm, naked chest. And her body fit perfectly against his. As though it was meant to be in that exact place. Next to Finley. Warm skin against warm skin.

Time once again moved outside of her awareness and instead of sitting on the ground, she was standing with the support of the wall and Finley's arm. Finley was standing up as well. Except now, they stood facing each other.

Maggie settled into the new position with her shoulders pressed against the wall, and then Finley was sliding down her body to his knees.

His lips grazed her navel and her body shuddered in anticipation. His hands slipped from her waist to her hips and he added to her support.

Which turned out to be a good thing because his mouth moved lower and his tongue flicked against her clit.

All thoughts left her brain. Gone was the idea that she caused a man's death. No more arguments with her animal. She didn't care about any of that. The only thing that mattered was the wonderful tickling that threatened to completely overwhelm her.

Strong hands slid down to her thighs and spread her legs further apart. She was so wet. As much as she wished she could blame the shower, she knew better. His tongue ran the length of her slit, lapping up her juices, and his thumb pressed against her clit at the same time.

Too many sensations invaded at once, overwhelming her with pleasure.

A whimper echoed against the tiled walls. She thought the sound came from her, but couldn't be certain. Reason and logic left, and all that remained was pleasure and desire. Not knowing what else to do with her hands, she slapped them against the wall. When that wasn't enough, her fingers combed through his now shower-wet hair, holding him in place in case he had any bright ideas of moving away.

In the past few days, Maggie experienced a broad swath of new experiences, and she loved that Finley was the one leading her along this new path.

The whimpers shifted into moans. Moans that grew louder. She wanted to feel him inside her again, but all the tugging and pulling didn't budge Finley from his current task. The male's mouth was a master at bringing her to the cusp of an orgasm, but holding her back from falling over the edge.

Just when she thought his mouth and thumb were the pinnacle of pleasure, Finley slipped a finger into her, stretching her in new and exciting ways as his lips wrapped around her clit. A second finger joined the first and her body responded by tightening around him as he slid his fingers in and out of her wetness. His teeth, tongue, and lips attacked her clit while his fingers coaxed her to brand new levels of pleasure.

Her fingers tightened their grip on his hair and she wiggled her hips, attempting to close her legs and alleviate the pressure growing between them. She was so close, but his shoulders blocked her.

"Finley!" Her head fell back as she moaned out his name.

He twisted his hand and curled his fingers while sucking harder on her clit.

Everything came together, and she exploded. Her back arched, rocketing her off the wall. The only thing keeping her bucking hips from throwing Finley off her was his arm wrapped around her waist, holding Maggie close to him.

Her moans and scream accompanied her writhing as her orgasm took over her body and rolled through her. His fingers slipped free as he continued to lap at her arousal. Once satisfied, he kissed his way back up her body, still trembling from the orgasm.

When Finley's mouth found hers, she didn't pull away or turn her head. She kissed him with the same ferocity of the orgasm he gave her. His free arm wrapped around her shoulder and pulled her against him.

The comfort from his arms embraced her, and she closed her eyes and settled against him.

They stood together, under the cooling water of the shower, in silence. Neither moved, not wanting to break the peaceful moment. When the water turned too cold to stand, Finley pressed his lips to a spot on her neck, just above her shoulder.

"You're mine, Pocket." He reached behind him and turned off the water, then grabbed a towel and wrapped it around her before taking a towel for himself. "You're my mate, Maggie, and you belong here, with us, in Broken Peak. I didn't think I could handle having a mate here, but after tonight, I don't think I can handle *not* having you here."

The pleasure numbed her brain, and she nodded along with his words. "My dad. I want my dad here."

"Anything, Pocket. I'll do anything for you. And if you want your dad, I'll get you your dad."

Maggie hadn't completely figured out the mating thing yet or how she'd explain to Finley why she'd have to go away until she was sure the Gaze wouldn't come after her. But that could come later. For now, she'd enjoy what she had with him.

CHAPTER TWENTY

BRAY leaned back in his chair and peered across the top of his desk at Finley. When Finley found both Alphas in Bray's office he considered himself lucky. He hadn't realized that they'd do a better job at convincing him he shouldn't head to Moundsville that afternoon together than alone.

"I don't care what your contact says, Vixen. She's convinced her dad isn't safe, and after everything Leighton shared, I don't disagree. I promised her I would get her father and I'm going."

"Moundsville isn't safe, Finley."

"I know, but her dad's there and if you don't think she's gonna rabbit in a few days, you all are crazy."

"You aren't going alone." Vixen didn't outright forbid him. That had to count for something. "The reasons why you want to get her father out of there are the same reasons Bray and I aren't comfortable sending you out there alone."

"Fine, we can use your contact to help."

Vixen waved a dismissive hand at his suggestion. "Will's not a shifter. And he's a non-combative. I have a small team, all retired from the Navy, they can help, but it will take a few days to round them up, explain the situation, and see if they're even interested."

Bray released a loud sigh. "They're humans. Even if they're elite, a group of shifters, yes even raccoon shifters, can overpower them in the right situation."

Vixen looked away from them and stared at the wall with a cork board covered with bills, notes, and all the other minutia of the day-to-day running of the Pack. The things Bray tried to teach them, but didn't hold half the excitement of Vixen's training. "If everything Mac knows is true and all of Leighton's information is correct, we'll be opening ourselves up to a second battlefront."

"Then Maggie and I will leave. We'll head away from Broken Peak. If we aren't here, they can't blame you."

"Not acceptable." Bray shook his head in disagreement. "Vixen wasn't giving you a reason why you couldn't go. This is how she thinks things through."

Finley's eyes widened. In the abstract he understood she worked things out, he just never expected to witness it. Every time she issued directives and orders, she'd already worked through all the variables. Finley wasn't sure he liked seeing her at work. It took away from her legend and their underlying belief in her infallibility.

A fallible Vixen was a frightening concept.

"Okay, so let us go for a visit with her father." Finley leaned against the wall and crossed his arms over his chest. "She's not gonna like it, but she'll be less likely to rabbit."

"Fair enough. Leave first thing in the morning and bring Tevin with you. That will give Will and Danielle enough time to send her dad a message. He's being watched when he leaves the territory, but they're lax inside the compound. We know there are at least three safe areas in the compound where there's no surveillance. But we need some time to get the message to Will to pass on to her dad."

"No way. Tevin is not coming with us."

"He's good in a fight, if it comes to that," Bray said.

"He'll whine the entire time and Maggie will bite his face off at the first opportunity."

"Fine, Allard then, but bring the General too."

"He's here?" Finley hadn't seen the old man at the Lodge in days, but he wouldn't mind having the older man around. Hell, he'd even take Tevin if the General came along.

"He just got back this morning." Vixen answered, but offered no explanation as to where General Jesup had been. The two of them were working on a side project, whatever that was, that caused the General to come and go at random. "Think Maggie will be able to wait until tomorrow morning?"

Finley's head bobbed up and down in agreement. He'd have to find a way to distract Maggie for the night, but that could end up being fun for the both of them. "Early though? Maggie's raccoon is growing as impatient as she is."

"There's another consideration." Bray looked away from Finley. "If the bond is fading, her father is going to be sick."

"We'll deal with that if it happens."

Bray and Vixen shared a look. Entire paragraphs were spoken back and forth in complete silence. It was bad enough that no one could hear their conversations, but somehow their lack of expression made it worse. There was no reading of body language to get the gist of the conversation either. All Finley could figure was that it was something bad. Especially if they hadn't said anything sooner.

"What aren't you telling me?"

Vixen waited until Bray nodded, but didn't look at Finley when she finally spoke. "Will's noticed that her father is looking worse. At first he suspected poison, but we ruled it out."

"Okay, so instead of a visit, it becomes an extraction."

"An extraction might not be possible though. Not if he's as weak as Will thinks, and not if the bond is still there." Bray delivered the second wave of bad news.

"But we have Mac and Eleanor. Between the two of him, we have a better chance of helping him survive the bond breaking. And if he's as sick as he is, then the Gaze will kill him for sure when it's faded enough."

"Extracting him is a last recourse option, and only if the General agrees. This isn't a rescue mission. It's recognizance."

Finley opened his mouth to protest, but Vixen cut him off with a sharp wave of her hand. "We're not saying a rescue mission isn't going to happen, but this is a quick there and back mission so Maggie gets eye's on confirmation that her father is as okay as can be expected. A rescue mission will put her in danger, Finley. She'll be rash and she won't listen to her raccoon when it matters most."

"What do you mean, listen to her raccoon?" The flood of new information overwhelmed Finley, and he wasn't sure what piece to focus on first.

Bray lifted a shoulder, "just in the theory stages now. But her raccoon seems to have more influence over her than our wolves have over us. It might be a side effect from the amount of time she spent as her animal.

"Or it might be something else." Vixen added. "Speaking of her raccoon, that animal's quite the fighter. Think she'd agree to joining the patrols?"

"She would, but I wouldn't."

"Take it from me, you won't be able to stop her if it's something she wants to do." Bray rolled his eyes at Finley's protest. "We can start our very own club. It will be great. We can even have a secret handshake and matching jackets."

"She's not a wolf. Or a bear or a mountain lion. She's not like the rest of us."

"No, she's not anything like the rest of us. She's something else entirely, even if she hasn't accepted it yet." Vixen's eyes flared an eerie golden color as she spoke about Maggie. "If she agrees, I'll add her to the patrols. But only as a third. Maybe we'll send her out with Gareth's clan."

"You know she doesn't buy into the idea of the prophecy at all, right? And every time you try to convince her that this is all part of some grand plan, she digs her heels in and sticks her fingers in her ears. She's almost as bad as Foster when he doesn't want to hear something, like Eleanor telling him it's time for bed."

Vixen shrugged. Apparently Maggie's thoughts didn't matter one bit to her. Before saying anything that would get himself in to trouble, Finley shut his mouth.

"Wise male," Bray grinned and winked at him. "Go find Allard and let him know you're leaving for Moundsville in the morning and tell Maggie before she takes a runner. Vi or I will take care of informing the General."

"Thanks."

"No need. If it keeps Maggie with us and helps her decide to stay, I'm all for it."

Bray glared at Vixen and her choice of blunt words. "This was always part of the plan, Finley. That we're moving up the timetable isn't a reason for thanks."

Finley backed out of the office and placed his hand on the heavy door. "Want me to–"

"Please." Bray continued to glare at his mate. "Vi, you need to learn that blunt words aren't always the best–"

Finley closed the door. Not that Bray and Vixen ever really argued, but witnessing any chinks in their relationship weirded Finley the hell out. Besides, he had to find Maggie and tell her the news.

It turned out she wasn't difficult to find. Maggie was sitting at the kitchen table and staring at a small box in front of her.

"What's that?" Finley nodded at the box.

"Hmm?" She lifted her head, but quickly looked away from him.

She was too late. Finley noticed her shame-faced expression and didn't have to think very hard for the reason for her guilt.

Maggie was planning on bolting.

"What's that?" Finley sat next to her and slid the box across the table, closer to him.

"Oh, a box." Her fingers tugged at the hem of her shirt, needing something to do.

"Yeah, what's in it?"

"Things."

Finley released a loud sigh. "Maggie."

"It's things my raccoon took. I need to return them."

Finley pushed the box away and picked up her hand. "Unless it's something valuable, no one really cares. I mean, as long as you don't have a bunch of Foster's toys in there. Or Hampstead."

Maggie turned her face away and lowered her gaze.

"You don't have Hampstead in there, do you?"

"No."

Finley squeezed her hand. "What would you say about a trip to Moundsville?"

"Are we getting my dad?" The box and its contents were forgotten, and she immediately perked up at the suggestion.

"No, it's not the right time. This is just a visit. But Vixen promised me we'd get your dad out of there. She's already working on a plan."

Maggie jumped to her feet and would have run out of the kitchen if Finley didn't still have a tight grip on her hand. He tugged her back, and she landed on his lap in an undignified heap. Not that he minded. He liked the way she fit perfectly against his body, no matter where they were.

"Pocket?" He brushed away a stray curl of hair and pushed it behind her ear.

She tilted her head back and looked up at him with a broad smile.

"Promise me you won't run without telling me. Because even if you do manage to run, I will find you and I'll land wherever you land. You aren't human like Danielle or Eleanor, you understand that we're mates and distance isn't going to stop us being mates."

She closed her eyes and nodded. Maggie didn't say anything, but then she wasn't the type of female who ever admitted fault. He liked that about her. Hell, he *loved* that about her. The more he considered it, he realized there were a lot of things he loved about Maggie. Her independence and ingenuity were just a few of the things he could list off the top of his head.

"I love you, Pocket."

Her eyes widened. It didn't take a genius to figure out mating and love were anathema to each other in Gazes.

"You don't have to say it back, but I want you to know that I love you. I'd love you even if we weren't mates." He kissed the tip of her nose. "Now, go put that box back while I find Allard and let him know he's coming with us on a field trip."

CHAPTER TWENTY-ONE

MAGGIE knew the way to the garage as well as she knew the trees with the best hidey holes in the woods bordering the Lodge. Finley's pack had been welcoming and generous, allowing both Maggie and her raccoon free rein to explore the surrounding territory at her whim. It was a stark contrast to life with the Gaze where sneaking away was part and parcel with life if she wanted anytime by herself.

Our pack.

"No, not ours. His." Maggie resorted to speaking with her raccoon, not having to keep it secret around the wolves and Vixen's griffin.

He's our mate, and the pack is ours.

"We're not arguing about this." She stepped into the massive garage and stopped just inside to look for Finley.

"Not arguing about what?" Allard peeked around a large black Range Rover.

"Nothing." Maggie waved away the question with a dismissive hand, much the same way she'd seen Vixen do when the Alpha didn't want to answer questions. It must have worked because Allard shrugged and resumed packing the car with large cases. "What's that?"

"Preventative measures." Allard hoisted another case into the back of the SUV.

Maggie rounded the vehicle and peered into the cargo area. Five large cases sat perfectly stacked in the back. "That's a lot of preventative measures."

"Vixen doesn't like to take chances. Speaking of which," Finley joined Allard and Maggie at the back of the SUV and tossed a small nylon bag to her, "put those on."

Maggie opened the bag and looked inside, but only found a small pile of fabric. "What is it?"

"Body armor, like we wear on patrol. It won't stop a bullet, but it will slow one down." Allard answered and paused his packing to pluck at the collar of his long-sleeved black shirt. "We all wear them when we leave pack territory."

"And usually on patrols. Except they're a pain in the ass to get out of when you have to shift in a hurry and our wolves hate them." Finley added.

She shrugged and stepped between the open front and back doors to change shirts. Modesty wasn't that big of a deal to her any longer. Her comfort with the pack had made it possible to strip in front of them before shifting without having to worry about any unwanted leering looks. But moving away from Allard was for Finley's benefit. Both he and his wolf spent a good fifteen minutes growling because someone other than him could have seen her naked.

As soon as the shirt was on, she understood why the wolves didn't like the clothes. The shirt was tight to her skin and heavier. It was like wearing a heavy wool sweater, but without the bulk. She wiggled around until the fabric settled less uncomfortably against her skin.

"This sucks."

"Yep. But don't say that around Tevin or you'll get an hour-long lecture on just why we don't need them and listing everything wrong with them in extreme detail." Finley grinned as he appeared next to her and smoothed the fabric down her back.

"Come on, let's go. Danielle heard from Will, Maggie's dad will meet us in five hours. We'll have to make up time on the drive." General Jesup, an older human Maggie had met a few times, but never spent any time with, arrived at the garage and climbed into the backseat.

Maggie pointed at the General and leaned in close to Finley to whisper, "he's coming too?"

"Yes, Maggie, I'm coming too. Get in the car, we need to get on our way or we'll miss the meetup."

"You get used to him and he's worth having along." Finley looked away from her to hide his grin. "Get in, Pocket."

Maggie shrugged and climbed into the backseat next to the General. As long as she got to see her father, she didn't care if Vixen came with them. Finley closed her door and circled around the front of the car to the driver's side. Maggie watched his easy lope and the movement of his muscular body with an appreciation that the General noted if his mocking smile was anything to go by. Allard slammed the back closed and was sitting in the front passenger seat by the time Finley sat behind the steering wheel and started the car.

"Let's go." Allard closed his eyes and leaned his head back against the headrest. "I can get a four hour nap in to make up for my lack of sleep."

"You weren't on a late patrol last night. Gareth's clan took that shift."

"But I was up before the ass crack of dawn. I want a nap." Allard crossed his arms over his chest, as though the gesture made his point.

Finley pulled out of the garage and onto the old lumber trail. "Fine, be a princess."

"The smartest operatives sleep at any opportunity." The General mimicked Allard's pose, complete with the same tilt of the head with his chin tucked close to his chest.

"Yeah, but we aren't operatives." Maggie grabbed hold of the oh shit handle as the SUV bumped along the uneven ridge filled dirt road.

"We're always operatives, Maggie." The General replied.

Maggie rolled her eyes and settled in for a long ride. "You know, this went much faster when I was the one driving."

"You also almost got caught at a rest stop. I'm not sure your trip is the best standard all other trips should be compared to." The General raised an eyebrow, but kept his eyes closed. It was freaky looking as hell. The old soldier probably practiced it in front of a mirror for years before perfecting it.

Maggie leaned forward between the front seats and smacked Finley's shoulder with the back of her hand. "What did you do? Rent out space on a billboard and tell everyone?"

"Ow." Finley took his hand off the wheel and rubbed his arm. "No, Danielle heard the story too. She's the resident town crier and broadcasts everything."

"Yeah, well..." There wasn't much Maggie could say to Finley's answer.

"Assume anything you tell her will be known by everyone within minutes. She's a good way to get news out if you don't want to have to tell everyone yourself." The General supplied.

Maggie turned to the old man, tilted her head to the side and stared at him for a moment. "Can I ask you a question?"

"You just did."

Maggie rolled her eyes up to the ceiling of the SUV and groaned. "You know what I meant."

"What do you want to know?" His eyes remained closed, but Maggie noted the hint of a smile on his lips. At least she hadn't pissed him off.

"Why are you here?"

"In the car with you? Or are you asking in a more general way?"

"General." She waved away his question with a brush of her hand. What other way would she have meant?

"It's a long story, but the summation is that as much as Vixen has claimed the Pack and those tied to the Pack as hers, she's mine. If maintaining her safety means I have to spend time with the Pack, then I will."

"We have at least four hours. Give me the long story."

The General sighed, but began from the beginning, long before Vixen was ever one of the Alphas of Broken Peak Pack.

Four and a half hours later, the General finished his story just as Finley pulled into an open area on the edge of the compound's territory.

Maggie leaned between the front seats and peered out the windshield. "Where is he?"

"We're early. Give him a few minutes." Allard grumbled at the nosy raccoon shifter invading his space.

Finley reached across the console and pulled a deck of cards from the glove compartment. "How about a game of cards while we wait?"

"Poker?" Maggie leaned back in her seat.

"No." Finley and Allard responded together.

"You cheat." The General grinned.

"No, I don't!" She protested.

"You do, we just haven't caught you yet. But there's no way anyone should win as many hands as you manage." Finley winked at her, softening the accusation.

"Fine. Go Fish?"

"You'll still probably cheat. Let's just play Bull Shit, at least the point of the game is to cheat." Allard suggested.

They finished their first game and were just starting their second when a movement from the woods caught in Maggie's peripheral. She turned her head to look out the window and gasped. The man approaching the vehicle was a shadow of her father. His normally thick brown hair was limp and grey. When she had left, her father had at least appeared healthy, but there was nothing healthy about his waxy skin or jaundiced eyes. A month hadn't even passed.

At some point between seeing her father and opening the door of the car, Maggie made a decision. Her father was coming home with her. She glossed over the word home. There would be time enough to come back to it later. But right at that moment, the only thing Maggie cared about was her father.

She ran up to him and wrapped her arm around his waist. Her father had always been a slight man, but he weighed half as much as he did when she ran away. Worse, it didn't take much to support and guide him back to the SUV.

Finley, Allard, and the General stood outside the Range Rover and stared into the woods. All three were armed.

When had that happened and where had the guns come from?

Maggie shook those thoughts free. They didn't offer any help.

She pushed her father into the backseat. But before climbing in with him, she stood on the running board and looked over the top of the SUV at Finley. "If you really care for me. Even a little. You'll get in and drive home. Now."

Finley nodded and backed up to the SUV. Both Allard and the General jumped on the running board, but stayed outside, keeping their guns trained at the woods.

"Get in." Finley shifted the SUV into reverse and was already backing up before she had even settled onto the backseat. As soon as the door closed, Allard slapped the roof of the car and Finley's foot slammed down on the accelerator.

The SUV careened along the dirt road in reverse, but neither the General nor Allard moved from their perch. Once the wheels hit pavement, Finley yanked the wheel and threw the SUV into drive. Tires screeched and the stench of rubber invaded the cabin of the vehicle. Allard climbed into the car first and once his door closed, the General followed.

"I spotted three."

Maggie looked around her father at the General. "What?"

He ignored her question, instead he sent a text on his phone.

"I saw three too, but I think there were at least five more." Finley shifted his stare from between the rear-view mirror and the front windshield. "I don't think they're following us."

Allard glanced over his shoulder between the front seats and stared at her father for a moment before turning his attention to the phone in his hands. "Mac?"

"Mac," Finley agreed. "And Eleanor, too."

"Margret," her father looked over at her. "What did you do? Your mother…"

"Fuck Mother. She gave birth to me, but that's where the mother thing stops. She's never been my mom, and she's not your mate either. Not the way mates are supposed to be." If anything, Maggie's time with the Pack taught her how mates should be. And whatever her mother and Dad were, they weren't mates.

"I need to go back."

"No. You don't. What you need to get the hell away from here and the hell away from mother."

"She could die."

"I don't care and neither should you. She doesn't give a fuck about you."

"Vixen says to drive straight up to Mac's. Use the logging trail."

As the conversations flew around her, two uncomfortable thoughts settled heavily on her. The first was why were they telling Vixen and the second was why was Vixen giving orders. At some level she understood her experiences with Zachery and the Gaze shaped her reaction, but after seeing her father's condition, rationality wasn't part of her thought process.

"Why is Vixen saying to go to Mac's? And is that why you came? So you could spy for Vixen."

The General cleared his throat. The old man nailed the attention grabbing noise that was the equivalent of pouring cold water on someone. "I'm not here as a spy. I'm here because you needed a third man in case this visit turned sideways, which it definitely did. And Allard isn't calling to let Vixen know what's happening, he's calling because this is a lot more complicated than a snatch and grab when it wasn't supposed to be one."

"He'll die if he stays with the Gaze."

"And he could die away from his mate. I'm trying to make sure that doesn't happen. You don't have to trust me, Maggie, you just have to trust Finley. He trusts me."

Maggie spent the rest of the ride home stewing in her pout and ignoring everyone else in the Range Rover. Even her father, who was still making feeble protests before finally falling asleep an hour and a half away from War. The jostling from the uneven logging road didn't even wake him.

Mac, Vixen, and Bray met them in the clearing about twenty yards away from Mac's cabin and swept her father away as soon as the SUV came to a stop. Maggie trotted after them, but Finley came up behind her and wrapped his arms around her waist. He scooped her up against him and held her close.

"Let them take care of it, Pocket."

The General got behind the wheel of the SUV. "Take her back to the Lodge. I'll take care of the vehicle and let Will know what's going on."

The SUV crept back down the hill toward the garage, but Maggie didn't care about anything happening around her. The only concern her brain focused on was her father's well-being and why Finley stopped her from following them.

Finley hoisted her under his arm and headed back to the lodge. At some point, Maggie decided the silent treatment was the best punishment for Finley, but didn't inform him because that defeated the purpose of the silent treatment.

Once at the Lodge, Finley set her down on the porch. "Don't run off, Pocket. I'll chase you and it won't be fun for either of us."

"You'll have to catch me first." But she didn't say the words because of the whole silent treatment thing. Instead, she thought them.

"Eleanor hasn't found anything yet, but Leighton headed over. He's the only one with direct experience with broken bonds, not killing a mate." Danielle peeked her head out the front door. She took one look at Maggie, silently stomping back and forth along the length of the porch, and grinned at Finley. "She needs to be angry, don't try to fix it. She doesn't want it fixed."

"But..." Finley stared at her back, but she avoided looking at him.

"Let her be angry. She's not angry at you, but she will be if you try to fix it."

Maggie was finished with listening to them talk about her and stomped down the porch to the yard. She didn't need to look behind her to know Finley followed.

"What are you doing? We just said don't try to fix it." Allard hollered, but Finley didn't respond and Maggie didn't dare look behind in case the sight of Finley sapped her anger.

CHAPTER TWENTY-TWO

FINLEY kept Maggie from Mac's cabin for exactly thirteen hours and twenty-eight minutes. Since he figured she'd sneak out in the middle of the night, he was pleasantly surprised that she bothered waking him up in the morning at the ass crack of dawn, as Allard liked to call it.

"I'm leaving in five minutes."

Finley opened one eye, then the second. "To go…?"

"To Mac's. Where else would I go?" She flopped down on the side of the bed and fell to her back, spreading her body across the foot of the bed.

"I didn't know. You haven't said anything to me since we got back to Broken Peak last night."

"Yeah. I wasn't talking to you."

"I know." Finley pressed up on his elbows and smiled at her. "Care to tell me why?"

"I'll tell you while you're getting dressed."

Finley didn't hesitate for more than thirty seconds before jumping out of bed and hurrying to his dresser to grab the first jeans and shirt his hands touched.

"I was angry."

"I figured. But what did I do?"

"Nothing. And everything. My dad is dying, and we all know it, and..."

"And I was there, stopping you from being there in case he died last night?" Finley guessed.

"What if he had died last night? You saw him, Finley."

"He didn't though. Mac is like the wise man of shifters. If anyone can help your dad, it's Mac. And Leighton's mom left, breaking the bond with his father, but his father lived. Eleanor has access to all these journals written by shifters hundreds of years ago. There couldn't be a better place for him, but if you were there, you'd get in the way."

"Vixen and Bray went to Mac's."

Finley pulled the shirt down over his head and bent forward so he could see Maggie's face. "Vixen isn't normal. The whole griffin thing aside, she has powers none of us have seen before. If all the wisdom failed, there was the chance Vixen could force him to live."

Maggie's nose wrinkled as she stared back up at him with unblinking eyes. "Really?"

"Yep. She can make a lot of things happen that shouldn't."

"Okay." Just like that, Maggie accepted his explanation. "But why didn't you tell me this last night?"

"Would you have listened last night?" Finley pulled on a pair of socks and boots.

"Fair point." They both know she wouldn't have listened, but they didn't need to expand on it.

"Let's go, Pocket." Finley held his hand out to her and pulled Maggie to her feet when her fingers wrapped around his. On their way out the door, Finley grabbed Maggie's book from the dresser.

At Mac's, Finley let Maggie go inside alone. He wasn't any help in the matter of broken bonds, and besides, Maggie needed the time alone with her father. Finley settled into one of the chairs on the porch and opened the book to the second chapter, *The Bee Eater*. He didn't think it would be his favorite book, being rather on the dry side, but it was kind of interesting.

Thirty minutes later, Maggie stepped out of Mac's cabin and wiped her hands across her cheeks, to hide her tears. The meeting must not have gone as well as expected. Instead of pulling her into his lap and comforting her, like his wolf wanted him to do, Finley stood up and began undressing.

"What are you doing?"

"Let's let our animals run."

She waited all of ten seconds before her clothes came off and a little raccoon was chittering away, impatient that Finley hadn't yet shifted.

"Okay, so it looks like we're all in agreement then." Finley finished undressing with a huge smile and his wolf was ready to go.

The shift was quick, painless, and without any flash of lights or sparkles. Though Danielle threatened Leighton with creating a pyrotechnic display to accompany his shifts because shifts should be full of magic and sparkles according to her. All the shifters in Broken Peak took great pride in the fact that their lives were nothing like the shifters from movies and TV shows, but Danielle had been on a mission to "give them all a little more bling" since she arrived.

As soon as his wolf stood in front of the little raccoon, he rubbed his snout against her. The raccoon basked in the affection and reached out to Finley's wolf with her grippy little paws. But just like Maggie didn't need Finley's comforting, her raccoon didn't need comfort from his wolf. The raccoon spun and waddled away as fast as her little legs moved and Finley's wolf gave chase.

They ran and played through the woods. The raccoon climbed trees and kept pace with the wolf by jumping from branch to branch. The wolf slowed his pace and showed the raccoon his favorite places. The raccoon sat on the edge of the river and caught small fishes, which she immediately offered to the wolf.

A few hours later and back at the Lodge, an exhausted Maggie curled up against Finley in his bed.

It wasn't a good day for Maggie, but it was better than then when she stepped out of Mac's cabin after the visit with her father.

For three days, they followed the same routine. Visit Mac's, let their animals run, then back to the lodge where Maggie found comfort with Finley.

It might not have been the best of conditions and Finley wasn't planning on pressing the matter, but the time to claim Maggie couldn't come soon enough for his wolf. Or him.

On the fourth day, Maggie ignored Finley's invitation to shift and walked away from him. He found her curled up in his bed.

"Pocket?" Finley closed and locked the door behind him. He slipped into bed with her and wrapped himself around her body. "Wanna talk about it?"

"He's not strong enough to survive. He looks worse every time I visit." It had to have been bad for her to share so quickly.

He stroked her hair and back while stalling for time to come up with the right words, which was impossible. There were no right words for watching a parent wither away and die. "Mac says it's about who is stronger, man or animal. If his animal is stronger, the broken bond will destroy him. If the man is stronger, you'll be reason enough for him to survive. And Leighton says it gets a lot worse before it gets better."

"It's never going to get better though."

"You don't know that, Pocket. If it was a lost cause, Mac and Leighton would have said as much, but they haven't. So there's still hope. You just have to keep that hope going when you visit. Remind your father he's stronger than his animal." Finley kissed the top of her head.

She sniffled and wiped her nose across his shirt. "But how do I do that?"

"I don't know, Pocket, but we'll figure it out together."

CHAPTER TWENTY-THREE

A POUNDING

on the door woke both Finley and Maggie from their nap.

"Vi needs you." Bray's deep voice carried through the heavy wood. "Now."

Finley shot out of bed and reached for his shoes. "What's up?"

"I'm not yelling the details through the door. Bring Maggie too."

Finley looked over his shoulder at her, and his steady gaze sent a wave of warmth through her body. Completely inappropriate given everything that happened during the past few days, but her body didn't seem to care one bit.

"C'mon, Pocket."

The bed was comfortable, but Bray hadn't stopped knocking and even if Finley opened the door, Bray would probably continue making loud noises.

"Finnnne."

"Let's go. Before Bray knocks the door down."

Finley held out a pair of running shoes and she snatched them from his hand while rolling off the bed before it sucked her back in. She shoved her feet into the shoes and pulled her hair back in a ponytail. No way was there a brush made capable of wrestling her curls after a nap.

"Okay, okay. I'm ready."

Finley double checked before opening the door. "What's wrong?"

"We had visitors. They're at the shed."

Finley's eyes widened, and he reached out for Maggie, pulling her closer to him. "Really?"

Bray nodded.

"What's going on? What do you mean by visitors?" Maggie heard the same words as Finley, but had no idea what was being said.

"Who found them?" Finley ignored her questions.

"A few of Gareth's clan stumbled across them." So did Bray.

"How many?"

"Just get to the shed. Vi will give you a full report."

"You aren't coming?"

"We're doing sweeps in the woods."

Maggie's head ping-ponged between the two males as they talked, still not understanding a single thing they said.

"I should go with you?"

"No. Bring Maggie to Vi. We'll take care of the rest." Bray turned and walked away before Finley offered another protest.

"What's going on, Finley?"

"I'll fill you in on the way to the shed."

"Really?" She threw her hands in the air and stomped down the hall-way. "What is it with getting filled in on the way somewhere instead of right now?"

Foster barreled down the hallway with Eleanor fast on his heels, waving a stack of green cards in her hand. "No, you cannot visit Hampstead until you finish your sight words, Foster!"

Finley pulled Maggie aside before she got mowed over. "There are little ears here. Unless we know he's asleep, we don't talk about things in the living area of the Lodge."

Maggie watched Foster's blonde cowlick bounce as he bobbed and weaved down the hallway. "Fair point."

"These are all followers. Not a single one is an enforcer. None of them stood a chance."

The six bodies neatly laid out in front of the shed stared up at the sky with dead eyes. Apparently, the visitors Bray mentioned were all members of the Gaze. Zachery must have been pissed that they got her father away from him.

"Fanatics." Vixen leaned against the exterior of the wall of the shed, appearing unfazed by the number of bodies.

"What?" Maggie couldn't stop staring at the dead bodies.

"They're fanatics. Probably true believers."

"But why not enforcers? Zachery has a team of enforcers with combat skills."

"Finley took down three of them single-handedly. If he sent a team of enforcers here and none came back..." Vixen turned her stare toward Maggie.

"And word got out, he'd lose power." She filled in.

"So he sends fanatics. And when they fail, he doesn't lose strength."

"I think you're giving Zachery more credit than he deserves." Maggie ripped her stare away from the bodies. "To some extent, he's as much of a believer as his followers."

"Good." Vixen pushed off the wall.

"Good? Why is that good?"

"Then he'll do something stupid and we won't have to force it. The fanatics are malleable and disposable, but there will be a point where it will destroy his ego enough where he has to act. We'll be ready." Vixen opened the door to the shed. "Come on inside. The fanatics were disposable, but Zachery wasn't stupid enough to send them in on their own.

Maggie peeked around Vixen into the shed.

Martin, Zachery's head enforcer, sat tied to a heavy chair which appeared bolted to the floor. Unlike the others, he was very much alive. Bruised, swollen, and bloody, but still breathing.

"What's he doing here?" Maggie stepped inside the shed with Vixen and Finley right behind her.

She had expected Finley to stop her, but he let her go inside without protest.

"I found him running away after the others had been caught and killed."

Martin grinned at Maggie, exposing his bleeding mouth with a few missing teeth. "I'm here for Conrad. Zachery doesn't care if you're alive or dead, but he wants your father back."

Finley growled, but didn't move.

"Yes, yes, we know all this." Vixen rolled her eyes and waved her hand in a circle. "Maggie, you're welcome to stick around, but things are about to get messy. I'm done playing games."

Maggie looked up at Finley, who somehow managed to keep both Maggie and Martin in his line of vision. "Up to you, Pocket."

Whatever Vixen was capable of, Maggie wasn't sure she actually wanted to witness it.

"He's not worth it." Maggie turned and walked back outside with the already dead bodies, and Finley followed.

"It will get noisy. Why don't we go visit your dad instead?"

"No." Maggie looked straight ahead, avoiding the dead bodies. "I might not want to see it, but I'm not walking away from this."

For the first thirty minutes, she did her best to ignore the high-pitched screams and wailing.

Eventually she couldn't ignore the noises and tried covering her ears with her hands to block the screams.

Finley wrapped his arm around her shoulder and guided her away from the shed and the horrible noises coming from it.

"What's she doing in there?"

"It's better not knowing." Finley's eyes glazed over at some memory Maggie was glad she didn't know about. "Come on, she'll find us when she's done."

"What about the bodies? What will happen to them?"

"Again, it's better not knowing." Finley tucked her closer to him as they walked through the woods.

They walked together in silence, which was probably a good thing. Eventually they made their way back to the shed, which was quiet.

Vixen waited for them with her arms crossed over her chest as she stared down at the bodies. "They've been watching us."

Finley stopped several feet away and pulled Maggie closer and behind him, protecting her from what she wasn't entirely sure.

"They sent messages to the other gazes too." Vixen lifted her head and stared through Finley, right at Maggie. "He threatened Leighton's father, but we all know Leighton would probably thank him."

Finley shrugged in agreement. "What are you going to do?"

"Deliver a message." Vixen stared off into the woods, lost in thought for a moment. "Zachery also knows things he shouldn't. My former life, who the General is. He even knows Danielle and Eleanor's stories."

"I didn't tell them anything. I swear." Maggie peeked around Finley's body. Vixen wasn't asking her a direct question, but the insinuation was hard to miss. Vixen thought Maggie was reporting back to the Gaze.

"I didn't think you did, Maggie."

"My dad didn't either. He doesn't know anything."

"He knew enough to send you to War."

"To find Mac. Not you. He didn't know anything about you, and Mac wasn't more than a legend, but it got me out of Moundsville."

"Yeah, but if your dad knew about Mac, then so did other members of the gaze. Your father didn't have to say anything, if the story of Mac had been passed down. Mac isn't the first MacAllister in these parts." Vixen turned and walked away from them. "Come on."

"Where?" Finley asked, not letting Maggie budge from her place behind him.

"Back to the Lodge. We're going to have to yank this band-aid off and figure out how to adapt instead of waiting for something to happen."

Finley nodded in approval and stepped forward. Maggie hurried to catch up, but didn't want to say anything in case Vixen thought this was all Maggie's fault. Which, technically, it was.

"Whatever you're thinking, stop." Finley squeezed her hand.

"What does that even mean?" Maggie stared at the ground a few feet ahead of her instead of looking at anyone.

"It means stop thinking the way you are."

"How do you know what I'm thinking?"

"It's written all over your face."

Maggie didn't have any words and relied on a disgruntled noise instead.

"Two things you need to know. The Gaze won't give up, so neither can she."

"What's the second?" Maggie asked.

"If Vixen thought for a minute that you had anything to do with this, we'd both be dead."

"Both?" Maggie almost tripped over her feet, but Finley kept her from falling over with a firm hand supporting her.

"Well, she's strong enough to take whoever she wants out, but she'd have to go through me before she got to you?"

"I don't know if that's super sweet or super scary."

"Go with sweet. Sweet is better than scary." Vixen's voice called back to them.

"She has freakishly sensitive hearing too." Finley whispered and squeezed her hand. "Come on, the sooner we get back, the sooner you can witness Vixen's evil genius."

And the sooner Maggie could figure out how to keep the Pack safe from the Gaze.

CHAPTER TWENTY-FOUR

"WHAT'S going on?" Maggie peeked out from under the covers and stared at Finley as he moved around the room.

"I don't know. Allard and Leighton wanted to talk about something, probably patrols. As soon as we're done, I'll be back." Finley grinned at her in the mirror. Both he and his wolf loved seeing her in his bed. "It won't be long though."

Maggie nodded, "and what about Vixen? She left right after telling the pack what happened."

"Again–"

"Wait wait, don't tell me. I don't want to know, right?"

"Vixen is doing what Vixen is doing. She'll let us know what's happening when it's important. But my guess is she's delivering a message to Zachery."

"What kind of message?"

"The kind that involves dead bodies and is impossible to ignore."

Maggie considered his words for a moment. Whatever conclusion she came to seemed to satisfy her because she shrugged and moved on. "You'll come back soon?"

"Promise."

"Okay." She reached for a book on the bedside table and opened it to the page she marked. "I'll stay up then."

The lack of argument surprised Finley. It was all too easy. "You aren't saying you'll stay here now, but actually planning on sneaking out and spying on us, are you?"

"Noooo." Maggie shook her head dramatically, but kept her eyes glued to the pages of the book.

"Pocket…"

"Okay. Fine. I won't spy on you."

"Swear?"

Maggie rolled her eyes at him. Her shoulders fell, and the book dropped to her lap. "Fine. Yes, I swear."

"I'm holding you to it." Finley crossed the floor to the bed in a few steps and pressed his lips to her forehead. "Stay put, Pocket. I'll be back soon."

As he stepped out of the room, he looked back once. Maggie was nose deep in a book. Which was a good thing, or at least he hoped it was. With his Pocket he couldn't be sure she'd keep her promise if she thought she'd do more good following him.

He found Allard and Leighton in the kitchen. Both were sitting down with a jug of Mac's moonshine and three cups. "What's going on?"

"Sit down." Leighton poured the three cups full of the alcohol.

"Seriously, what's going on?" Finley stood behind a chair. He could wait them out for as long as he needed.

"Just sit, okay." Allard bent his head forward and pinched the bridge of his nose. "We need to talk and we can't do this without a lot of alcohol and with you standing up."

"Fine." Finley grumbled out a response and yanked out the chair before throwing his body into the chair and pulling a cup of moonshine to him.

Allard stared down at the cup he held in his hands. "So, we're just throwing this out there, but you know Maggie's your mate, right?"

"Yeah, I pretty much figured it out." Finley nodded. "Is that what this is about? You wanted to tell me Maggie's my mate?"

"Actually, no." Leighton tilted his head back and stared at the ceiling. "You're acting more like a bonded male. You hadn't even met her and you destroyed those three males from the Gaze sent to bring her back."

"What? No. What?" The words made no sense. No wolf bonded without claiming their mate, and Finley definitely hadn't claimed Maggie yet. He planned to, sure, but he hadn't claimed her and wouldn't without her permission.

Except it explained his reactions to everything since Vixen sent them to War to save an unknown shifter.

He lifted the cup and gulped down the alcohol. Yeah, Allard was right. They needed a lot of booze for this.

"Bonding without a claiming is unheard of. But it's not like Broken Peak is new to the impossible. First Vixen's griffin. Then there's Foster and the fact that Jackson knocked up a latent, I mean what are the chances of that happening since no one really believed in the idea of latents, anyway." Allard took a drink after finishing his justification why the impossible was possible, and probable when it came to Broken Peak.

Leighton added to the list, "and then along comes Dani who has single-handedly managed to create a safety net to protect us and other shifters."

"Are you really surprised your wolf would have bonded with the girl without claiming? In the scheme of things, this is probably the most possible of a long list of impossibilities we've all lived through, and it hasn't even been a full year since Vixen arrived."

Finley buried his hands in his face. "Shit."

"Yep. Shit." Leighton nodded. "But this might not be the first time it happened."

"What do you mean?" Finley peeked through his fingers at Leighton. "Wait. Hold on." He dropped his hands, lifted his head, closed his eyes, and sniffed at the air. No Maggie. She kept her promise. "Okay, she's still in our room."

Allard leaned back in his chair and shook his head at the sight. "I think this is more of a well fuck moment than a shit moment."

"Yep. Definitely fuck." Leighton agreed.

"What? Why?" Finley looked between Leighton and Allard.

"Dude, you just sensed where Maggie is. Dani and I bonded, I claimed her, and I still can't find her without actually looking for her."

"You are totally bonded." Allard nodded his head up and down.

"Definitely a well fuck moment." Finley rubbed the side of his face. "When you said this might not be the first time, what did you mean, Leighton?"

"Maybe my father's wolf bonded with my mom and there wasn't a claiming. Which totally explains why he only went even more bat-shit crazy instead of dying."

"Except that's not good news, is it?" Finley slumped in his chair and poured more moonshine into his cup.

"Well, if she leaves, you'll go crazy and either Vixen or Bray will have to put you down. But she won't leave."

"Yeah?"

"She won't leave." Allard agreed. "She could have left at any time, but stayed."

"She could have left in the middle of the night with her dad and no one would have stopped her."

"And she's still here. In your room. Not hers. Not that she really had her own room. You moved her in with you and she never protested. Not once."

"Yeah, okay, so she's a shifter, she gets the mate thing."

"No, you idiot, you two are bonded and never claimed each other. She came to War because this is where she's supposed to be because you're here!" Allard threw his hands up in the air in frustration that Finley wasn't getting it. "She's always been your mate! Before you even met her, she was your mate."

Well, fuck. How was he going to explain this to Maggie? Pocket had warmed up to the Pack, and he expected her to stay, but she ran hot and cold when they discussed mating. Her animal seemed all for it, but Maggie herself was hesitant unless they had just had sex. From everything he learned about the gazes, he didn't blame her though.

If she had done her usual thing, she could have overheard the conversation and Finley wouldn't have to be the one to tell her everything. He let his head fall back and rubbed the heels of his hands against his eyes.

Of all times to make her promise not to spy...

Finley sniffed at the air. He didn't believe he actually needed to sniff the air to sense it, but for whatever reason, it helped.

Pocket wasn't in the hallway, but Finley didn't know whether to be thankful or upset. He stretched his senses further down the hall to his room. Except she wasn't there either. He jumped to his feet, knocking the chair back with a loud enough crash for both Leighton and Allard to also jump up.

"What?" Both males half asked and half yelled at the same time.

"She's gone."

"What?"

"No. She's probably just lurking somewhere."

"She's not here." Finley shook his head slowly from side to side. The same feeling telling him she wasn't in his room let him know she wasn't anywhere in the Lodge. He didn't wait to hear any of their explanations and raced from the kitchen, down the main hall and out the front door.

Allard was only two steps behind. "Leighton's getting the others."

Finley skidded to a halt midway across the yard. His arms hung limply at his sides while he scanned the woods. He didn't know what he was looking for, but maybe his wolf did. He didn't hesitate with stripping and letting the animal out. The wolf took one step forward and swept his head back and forth across the woods.

When his wolf hunted, he did the same thing. Except now he wasn't looking for prey, he was tracking his mate.

A scream ripped through the night, but it wasn't one of fear or pain. It was one of anger. Vixen's griffin was there.

A heavy hand came down on Finley's head, holding him in place. The wolf leaned against Bray's leg, acknowledging his Alpha.

"She's searching. Neither Vixen nor the griffin are happy." Bray looked up at the sky. "Don't worry, she'll find her."

The wolf lifted his head and howled, joining the griffin's scream.

CHAPTER TWENTY-FIVE

MAGGIE hung from a branch by a rope tied to her wrists with her feet hovering a good foot above the ground.

She should have listened to Finley. He told her not to leave, but she got bored. Instead of sneaking down the hall and listening in on whatever the boys' meeting was about, she headed outside to visit her father. After all, going outside wasn't breaking her promise.

That's when Zachery caught her. She wasn't paying attention, and he grabbed her from behind as she took the long way to Mac's cabin.

Well, if this wasn't the definition of crap on a cracker, she didn't know what was.

And her shoulders ached too. Why couldn't Zachery, that turd nugget, tie her up in a less uncomfortable way?

The sharp scream cut through the night and the raccoon shifters standing in a circle around her looked around them for the source. They tried to be brave and not show their fear, but failed. Maggie didn't blame them. The noise scared the hell out of her too, and she knew its probable source, even if she hadn't seen it.

Vixen's griffin was out.

And hunting.

That meant they knew she was gone.

That meant Finley was probably looking for her too.

A howl joined the griffin's scream.

Yep. Finley's wolf was out too. She'd recognize that howl anywhere. "What was that?"

Maggie stared at the female who asked the question. Her mother. Except she wasn't her mother. Not really. Vixen was closer to a mom than her own mother. And her mother sure as hell didn't deserve her dad. Her dad didn't deserve the fate her mother dealt him.

And Finley didn't deserve that fate either.

He deserved a mate.

Finley deserved Maggie.

The realization hit her harder than Zachery's fist when it slammed into her cheek. And stomach. And kidney. And everywhere else he had hit her.

Maggie wouldn't turn into her mother. She wouldn't turn her back on Finley. It was time to accept that she was Finley's mate, and everything that came with it. The Pack, Vixen and Bray, Foster, and even Mac.

Okay, so she just needed to save herself, kill Zachery, her mother, and the three other enforcers who witnessed Zachery beating her, but didn't stop it. Sure, there were five other gaze members, but Maggie didn't think they were true believers like her mother. Zachery had brought them along to witness her punishment as a lesson.

She swung her weight back and forth while the griffin's screams distracted the raccoon shifters. Maybe, if she shifted her weight enough, she could get her feet on the tree. Just a little closer...

A tree cracked close to them. But it wasn't the sound of a branch snapping, it was the noise of a tree trunk breaking.

Maggie stopped her endeavors.

The Gaze members froze.

Except for Zachery. He stared into the woods behind her for a moment before lifting his chin at one of the enforcers. Before the enforcer took five steps, the trees behind her exploded.

Maggie twisted around until she could see behind her and wished she hadn't. The sharp griffin's beak yanked the spine right out of the enforcer's body.

That shouldn't have been possible.

And yet, Maggie was witnessing the griffin debone and disembowel the enforcer.

Once satisfied, the griffin stepped over the massacred body toward Maggie.

But it wasn't the griffin. It was Vixen.

Vixen with broad white wings and feathers instead of hair.

The griffin and women were one.

And then the griffin was gone, and the woman remained.

Vixen studied Maggie, quickly calculating each and every harm that had been done to her, before stalking towards Zachery. Who didn't have enough sense to step away from the approaching myth come to life who had just ripped the freakin' spine from a male!

The female Maggie no longer called her mother didn't have any sense either.

The other gaze members and enforcers did though and turned to run.

Except that was when the males of Broken Peak melted out of the woods and stopped their retreat.

Finley wasn't there. Maggie looked for him, but couldn't find him.

Bray stepped next to Maggie and wrapped his arm around her waist, supporting her weight and easing the ache of her shoulders. "We'll get you down from there in a minute."

"There are two rules you should know." Vixen's head cocked to the side as she stared at Zachery. Maggie imagined Vixen's eyes went birdlike too. "The first is there is always someone stronger in the room. When I'm there, it's me. And second. No one ever harms one hair on what's mine without paying the price. You're about to pay the price."

Maggie wasn't sure how it happened. One moment Vixen was standing in front of Zachery and the next she was behind him and snapped his neck. The unmistakable sound of breaking bones preceded the leader's body falling limp at her feet.

"Let that be a lesson to you all. If you want to live this fucked up life, that's fine. But if I hear about you going after anyone who wants to leave, I will hunt you down and this will seem like a walk through the Candy Rock mountains." Vixen swiveled her head around the area, looking pointedly at each of the Gaze members still breathing. Barely. Vixen's gaze landed on Maggie. "Did anyone else hurt you?"

Maggie's eyes bugged out of her head and threatened to fall out. At least between Bray and the rope still tied to her wrists, Maggie didn't have to worry about her knees giving out and collapsing like a fool in front of everyone.

"Did. Anyone. Else. Hurt. You?"

"Well, I'm scared to tell you now because, hollllllyyyy shiiiiiitttt!"

"Yeah, but just think how cool it is she's on your side." Bray reached up with a knife and cut the rope tied to the branch. "He'd be here, you know, but he shifted and his wolf won't let him shift back. We thought it was better not to have Finley's wolf add to the Vixen carnage. Danielle's doing her best to keep him distracted."

"Is he mad at me?" Maggie dropped to her feet and her arms fell, nearly causing a scream of pain as a fresh wave of aches pumped through her shoulders.

"Mad? No. Frustrated and annoyed, but not mad. Finley doesn't really know how to get angry. It's not in him." Bray untied the rope from her wrists and rubbed the marked skin until her circulation returned.

"That's an excellent trait for an Alpha, right?" Maggie planned on avoiding Vixen's question. She really didn't want to be responsible for anyone's death. Especially a death at Vixen's hands.

Bray laughed and swept his arm around at the Pack males, still standing in a perimeter around the Gaze members. Both dead and alive. "He won't be an Alpha for a long time. None of them will. In case you haven't figured it out, even with Mac spoon feeding it to you, Broken Peak Pack might have been sold to the wolf shifter community as a place for dominant wolves to grow into their Alphahood, but it's not that anymore. It's the pack of the women and females who are going to lead the shifters into whatever future Mac's convinced will happen. Maggie, you're a part of that, whether you believe it or not. You're as much a part of Broken Peak and its fate as anyone else."

"Maggie?" Vixen had enough of the conversation. "Who else hurt you?"

Maggie turned and looked at her mother. It would be so easy. Vixen was an armed weapon, and Maggie just had to point an aim. Except as horrible as her mother had been in that particular role, she was still a victim of Zachery and the twisted culture of the Gazes.

"Did she hurt you, Maggie?"

"No. Not in the way you're asking. Let her go. And let the others go." The temptation to say yes was powerful. But Maggie couldn't do it. And not because she was good, but because it would definitely kill her father. "If any of them come back, I will consider it as an intent to harm me."

Vixen grinned at Maggie, but it wasn't a friendly grin. It was a cruel grin. A hungry grin. The griffin wanted them to try it so she could destroy them the same way she'd destroyed the enforcer.

"Say what you need to whoever you want. And when you're ready, come back to the Lodge. Allard and Leighton will stick around to make sure no one does anything stupid, but they'll give you space." Bray smiled and patted her head.

The gesture should have pissed her off, but it didn't. She'd witnessed him doing the same thing to the males of the pack. He didn't do it to any of the women, though. Only her.

"Now, if you'll excuse me, I need to stop my mate from causing more carnage. She's going to owe Gareth big time if she expects him to clean this up."

Maggie watched Bray and Vixen fade into the woods and the other males melt into the darkness. But just as Bray promised, Leighton and Allard lingered. Just out of sight, but close enough for her raccoon to notice their presence.

"Margret."

"No. No. No." Maggie spun and faced the woman who said her name. "Leave. And don't ever come back. Next time I'll let Vixen kill you if I don't kill you myself."

A low growl came from the woods, but she couldn't tell if it was Leighton or Allard. All she knew was that it wasn't Finley.

"Just leave. All of you. Leave and don't ever come back." The Gaze, her mother, Zachery, they were all part of another life. A life she walked away from and never wanted to return to. Maggie turned and headed back to the Lodge.

And to Finley.

She took the quickest path back, but it was still a long walk. Alone, except for her guards. Vixen stepped out of the forest and onto the path next to Maggie, and her guards left, hurrying off to whatever tasks needed doing now that Vixen was there to keep Maggie safe.

"That was fast."

"It wasn't like there was anyone I really wanted to talk with."

"Finley is going to lose his shit when he sees your bruises."

Maggie sighed. "Yeah. I know."

"So, have you accepted it yet?"

"Accepted what? The whole being Finley's mate? Yeah, I'm good with it. Hanging from your arms and having a sadistic turd nugget using you as a punching bag sort of puts the mating thing into perspective."

"I didn't mean the mating, but you should be prepared that there's more to the mate thing. That can wait, though. What can't wait is whether you accepted your role."

Maggie didn't answer. So many things raced through her mind and she'd just severed ties with her Gaze in the most permanent way possible. The last thing she wanted was to be part of another group based on interpreted words.

Except this really wasn't the same, was it?

Vixen had power, but didn't take it and demand subjugation.

Eleanor didn't dictate how the words in the journals should be interpreted.

Danielle shared all her tricks with the Pack, because it was best for shifters in general and not just those living at Broken Peak.

When they neared the Lodge, Maggie still hadn't answered, but Danielle and Eleanor joined them.

"We would have met you sooner, but I don't do hiking unless I absolutely have to, and Eleanor finds me more entertaining to hang out with than Vixen."

"Aren't you supposed to be with Finley's wolf?"

"Allard and Bray are trying to convince him to shift and Leighton wanted me back inside, so we compromised and came to meet you."

Maggie nodded and the four women continued walking.

"There's supposed to be six of us, right?" Maggie asked.

"Yep," Eleanor answered.

Danielle rolled her eyes and blew her bangs out of her eyes. "Don't think too hard about it. Vixen and Mac have a plan and will let us know when they want us to. We didn't get filled in about you until you'd been here a few days. Was it as bloody as we all think it was?"

"Well, it wasn't exactly a peaceful gathering." Danielle's change of topic was rapid, but Maggie rolled with it.

"I've never seen her griffin pissed, but I heard about it. It's gruesome, right?"

"I'm right here, Danielle."

"Yeah, that's why I'm asking Maggie." Danielle's grin was unrepentant.

Maggie looked at the women with her. Well, the two women and the female. The prophecy Mac and Vixen were convinced would lead the shifters into the future had nothing to do with seeking power. It was about friendship. And family.

"Yeah, I accept it."

"Good."

The four women stepped out of the woods and into the yard in front of the Lodge, side by side. Danielle and Eleanor peeled off, went to their mates, and dragged them into the Lodge. Vixen squeezed Maggie's shoulder before walking across the yard. Bray and Tevin met her and walked off towards Mac's.

Finley was the only one remaining in the yard. But he was too far away. Her feet moved, walking at first, then breaking into a run, closing the distance between her and Finley. He didn't hesitate and ran to meet her. As soon as he was close enough, she jumped up and into his arms.

"I'm sorry."

"You okay?"

They both spoke at the same time.

"Yep."

"Don't be,"

And responded at the same time, too.

"Allard is with your dad. We can go there now, but I think you should clean up first. My wolf is going to lose it and I'm barely holding it together. Your father won't handle seeing you in this condition very well." Finley stroked his thumb across her bruised cheek and hissed.

"Shower with you. Bed with you. Then to see my dad in the morning. You didn't tell him what happened did you?"

"No. We didn't know what happened, just that you weren't in the Lodge."

"How did you find me so fast?" Maggie settled into his arms, resting her cheek against his chest.

"Yeah, about that, Broken Peak Pack has another impossibility to add to its list." Finley shifted her in his arms as he walked up the steps onto the porch and into the Lodge. "Apparently my wolf decided to bypass the whole claiming part of a mating and bonded with you."

"Really?" Maggie had never heard of a bonding happening without a shifter claiming their mate.

"Yeah. And Allard thinks you were always my mate. That our animals sort of made decisions irrespective of us."

Maggie laughed. That explained so much. Especially her raccoon's insistence that Finley was hers.

Finley looked down at her laughter. "You okay, Pocket?"

"Never been better." She nuzzled her lips against his neck. "But I think I would be even better after a shower. And bed. Your bed."

"Shower and bed, got it." He turned right and headed down the hallway toward the bedrooms.

CHAPTER TWENTY-SIX

MAGGIE stretched her arms up over her head and sighed happily in the bed. They promised the pack they'd go for a run to pick out a Christmas tree, but that was thirty minutes away.

Finley rolled to his side and looked down at her. Thirty minutes was more than enough time for what he had planned. He pounced. His lips found hers and he kissed her. Hard.

Her arms wrapped around his neck, pulling him closer. Her bruises had faded in the few days since the "incident" as everyone called it whenever Foster was close enough to hear, but she had still been tender. Even if she denied it, Finley knew about all her aches and pains. Finley was tempted to find a way to bring Zachery back so he could kill that bastard all over again. He shook those thoughts away. They had no business being there.

Their tongues met and all Finley's thoughts left his head.

Her kiss grew more urgent and his cock grew harder. He didn't care about anything except the way her soft body felt beneath him and her skin pressed against his.

"Finley..." Maggie moaned as his mouth found its way to the soft spot on her neck he wanted to mark. Their animals might have already bonded, but Finley still wanted to claim her. He wanted everyone to know she was his.

His body covered hers as he slid his lips down her chest to the swell of her breasts and then a nipple. When her back arched just so and a shudder ran through her body, his hands found her hips and he rolled them over until Finley was on his back and she straddled him.

Maggie looked down at him with a smile and rocked her hips forward. His fingers gripped her hips, holding her in place. "I need you, Maggie. I need you to be mine. All of you. Not just your animal."

Finley's wolf pushed towards the surface, agreeing with all of his words.

"I love you, Pocket. No matter the bond or the mating, I. Love. You."

He lifted her up and slid into slowly.

The sound of their shared moan filled the room.

Maggie leaned down and nibbled his ear. "I love you, too."

He couldn't wait. Maggie's words unlocked whatever had been holding him back. He rolled them again until he hovered above her, still moving in and out, slowly building both of their pleasure. The movement of her hips grew more urgent, but it was impossible to tell if she was pushing him closer to an orgasm or holding back her own.

Finley pulled out and rolled her to her hands and knees, taking her from behind with a force that pushed her across the bed. He was too close. He needed to come and needed her to come with him. From the growing volume of her moans and the way her body tightened and fluttered around his hard cock pounding into her, she was close. He reached beneath her and brushed his fingers across her clit. Her orgasm hit her hard, and he bent forward, biting her neck, just above her shoulder.

She screamed out in pleasure and Finley couldn't stop his orgasm. He fell forward, collapsing onto her back, but keeping his weight off her.

Finley wrapped his arms around her and pulled her tight against him as he rolled to his side. He licked at the bite mark, growling happily. She still needed to bite him, but that was another excuse to have great sex again. Maybe after the run.

He kissed the bite, his mark. "You're mine now, Pocket, just like I'm yours. Just like I've always been yours."

Maggie and Finley stood outside, waiting for the others. They made it outside with five minutes to spare and avoided any uncomfortable knocking at the door.

Foster, Eleanor, and Jackson were the first to join them. The rest quickly followed, and even Mac and Roose showed up.

The plan was to pick the tree out and then go for a pack run. A run everyone was looking forward to. Gareth's clan was out patrolling, but the mountain lions planned to join too. The plan didn't take Eleanor's brand of particularness into consideration. What should have taken them an hour at most turned into three hours.

One tree was tall enough, but not full enough. The trees with enough branches weren't tall enough. And then there was the debate about which held its needles better, a pine or fir.

Eventually, Eleanor found one that met all her requirements.

"Okay, pack run. Strip and shift!" Vixen called out before Eleanor could find a fault and prolong what was fast turning into an excruciatingly painful pack event. Almost as bad as Danielle's game nights.

While Eleanor fussed over Foster's shifting, the rest stripped off their clothes and let their animals out.

Maggie climbed onto Finley's back. Her stumpy little raccoon legs moved fast enough, but she didn't have the endurance to keep up with the rest of the pack for very long. Grabby little raccoon paws grabbed at his fur. Which distracted Eleanor long enough to let Foster shift without much more fuss.

Eleanor and Danielle climbed onto their mates' backs and they were off. The animals raced through the woods, weaving around the trees and leaping over fallen branches with Vixen leading the way in the sky.

As fearsome as the sight might have been to anyone watching, it was one filled with joy, but the run was short lived. Foster couldn't last for more than thirty or so minutes, and they'd already been out in the woods longer than planned.

Vixen guided them back to the Lodge and while the women laid out the clothing they collected when the others stripped, they all shifted back. Grabbing their clothes, they dressed and hurried inside.

No one wanted to risk Eleanor finding a reason to decide the tree wasn't perfect.

Finley grabbed Maggie's hand and pulled her back. He wanted a few minutes alone with her. He leaned down and kissed the mark he made on her neck.

"Do you feel different?" Finley asked. He understood he bonded with her, but wasn't sure what would happen once he claimed her.

Maggie nodded. "I feel whole. It's like something was missing, and now it's not. You?"

"Same, except I felt it the first time I saw you, standing there in our kitchen." He bent down and kissed her. "Come on. Dinner's waiting for us and so is your dad."

He wrapped his hand around her tiny hand and led her inside and to the kitchen.

Roose, Mac, Maggie's Dad, General Jesup, and the rest of the pack sat around the table. As soon as they sat down at the table, Mac cleared his throat and the quiet chatter stopped.

Mac hoisted his glass toward Vixen, "to the Hero!"

Vixen raised her glass to Eleanor, "the Sage."

Eleanor raised her glass to Danielle, "the Mage."

Danielle grinned and one upped everyone by standing up and raising her glass to Maggie, "the Rebel."

Maggie smiled at all of them and leaned against Finley, "to family."

"To family." The others echoed her toast.

Finley leaned back in his chair and looked around. It took a lot of years, but he finally had what he never realized was missing.

Family.

TURN THE PAGE FOR *BROKEN REBEL* EXTRAS, INCLUDING

The official, Jules Crisare-Sanctioned "What Kind of Shifter are You?" Quiz

An excerpt from the next Broken Peak novel, *BROKEN CROWN*

And More!

THE OFFICIAL "WHAT KIND OF SHIFTER ARE YOU?" QUIZ

You've read Broken Hero and laughed at the antics of the Broken Peak Pack and cheered when Bray claimed Vixen and accidentally on purpose released the Griffin lurking inside of her. Right? I mean maybe you didn't do all those things, but let's just pretend you have. Now, I bet you're wondering where you'd fit in the pack. Would you be a wolf shifter? Or a griffin shifter? Or maybe another kind of shifter entirely. Well, you no longer have to wonder. In the short time it takes you to answer the questions below, you'll find out what kind of shifter you are.

WHAT SHIFTER AM I?

(If you want to find out what kind of shifter your partner is, replace "you" with "he/she/they". Depending on the result, you might want to keep it to yourself.)

1. When Vixen and Bray invite you to a barbecue at Broken Peak, you:

    a. Hide in the woods and hope no one finds you

    b. Show up earlier and be the last to leave and drink the most moonshine

2. Vixen asks you to steal a shifter artifact from a private collector who refuses to sell (there's no chance of getting caught), you:

    a. Tell her no way

    b. Tell her sure, why not

3. Vixen thinks you should find a mate, you:

    a. Go out with whoever Mac recommends, and of course they're a perfect match, so you agree.

    b. Create profiles on shifter-r-us with the rest of Broken Peak Pack and go out on group dates so your friends can give you instant advice. Plus, if they don't like your friends, they aren't for you.

4. War passed a new ordinance, barring all concealed weapons, even daggers, you:

> a. Don't bring the dagger Vixen got for you into town and leave it at home instead

> b. Ignore the ordinance, besides it's not like you go to War all that often

5. After a long day chasing down false alarms that led no where followed by a double dose of training from Vixen, you just want to go home and fall into bed, but your best friend sends a text, asking if you want to go out for dinner in thirty minutes, you:

> a. Call them back right away, since you plan on venting and your best friend is a great listener

> b. Ignore the message and call your friend back the next morning, you plan on spending the night alone with your favorite book

6. While walking through the park late at night with no one around, you see a new "Keep Off Grass" sign, you:

> a. Complain to yourself, but avoid walking on the grass

> b. Yank the sign out, throw it into the trees, then gleefully hop around on the grass since there's no more sign to stop you

ANSWERS

1. a=1, b=0

3. a=0, b=1

4. a=1, b=0

5. a=0, b=1

6. a=1, b=0

Add up your points! Have the number? Great, now if you scored:

0-1 GRIFFIN
Always up for a group hunt or hanging out with the pack, even if it means exploring forbidden territory.

2 WOLF
You take every opportunity to spend time with your friend and pack and always obey your Alpha.

3-4 COYOTE
You don't mind occasionally hanging out with friends, but prefer to spend most of your time alone with your still and never let something like rules get in the way of doing something.

5-6 BEAR
You're the strong and silent type, always ready to help your few close friends you have as long as your aren't breaking any rules.

AN EXCERPT FROM THE NEXT BROKEN PEAK PACK NOVEL, *BROKEN CROWN*

Allard's hiding a secret. He's the firstborn son of a powerful Alpha fated for an arranged mating. When Delia shows up at Broken Peak, intent on convincing Allard to go through with the mating, Allard must face his past. There's only one problem ... Other packs want Delia. With Broken Peak Pack's safety in the balance, destiny and love confront the danger head on. Will Delia and Allard realize their fate in time? Or will Broken Peak lose its crown?

"DELIA."

Whoa.

Allard's voice was all low and growly. Nice and rough and totally unexpected from the refined voice she expected. "Allard."

Allard stepped down and moved closer to her.

Double whoa. Yeah, Allard was big. Delia had already come to that conclusion. What she hadn't realized was that Allard was one of those sexy guys who didn't know it, or maybe he did. Except he didn't bother to do anything to make himself sexier.

Worn jeans hugged his legs, not because the jeans were tight, but because his legs were just that muscular. And the worn flannel shirt, unbuttoned at the collar, was just snug enough to showcase his broad shoulders.

She wasn't sure what she expected exactly. After Allard ran off to the boondocks, his image stopped appearing in the social pages. But the male standing in front of her, with cheekbones that could cut glass, and a jawline only found on the photo-shopped cover of a magazine, wasn't even a glimmer in her imagination.

All things considered, being mated to Allard wouldn't be as bad as it could be. At the very least, if his personality turned out to be lacking, she could wear a pair of ear plugs and spend her time staring at him.

"I'm not sure what to say." There was his gravelly growl again.

Delia pushed her hair behind her ear and looked past his shoulder, anything not to stare at his face. "I know Vixen said we didn't have to mate, but I think you of all people should know what will happen if we don't complete the agreement."

"There are plenty of loopholes. And you might not know or trust Vixen yet, but I do, and if she says she won't force the terms of the agreement, then she won't. And she won't let my father, his pack, or the Council force the terms either."

"Allard, you haven't been out of pack politics that long." Delia swallowed the small lump in her throat, blinked back her tears, and turned to the male who she needed to convince to be her mate. "You know as well as I do that if I don't mate you, your father will try to get the Council to transfer the terms of the agreement to your brother. And they'll do it. The Council can't have a binding agreement between packs broken. We might as well make the best of it."

"You might want to read that agreement again. Besides, the Council doesn't have enough teeth to win a war against Vixen." Allard shoved his hands deep into his pockets and rocked back on his heels. "So, no, Delia. I'm not prepared to mate you. Or at least I won't until it's not because of some damn agreement made between our fathers before we were even born."

Allard turned his back to Delia, a brave move considering she had a dominant wolf inside her and was born an Alpha. But Delia wasn't considering pouncing on his back, she was too busy staring at his broad shoulders and the pleasant way his waist narrowed so his jeans hung just right on his hips and showcased one of the best asses she'd seen.

Wait.

What had he said about mating? Not the part about him not thinking he'd mate her, but that he wouldn't do it because of an agreement.

Did that mean he'd want to mate her for other reasons?

ACKNOWLEDGMENTS

Sitting down to write an acknowledgment page is much like making an acceptance speech at an award's show. It's more than likely that you will forget someone and then have to spend hours on the phone apologizing for the misstep. And God help you, if it's your mother. So, I should probably get that one out of the way first, right? I need to acknowledge my parents, especially my mother, who have supported me and define the phrase unconditional love.

The readers of the Broken Peak Pack and the Sentinels of the Silver Orb. Without them, Maggie and Finley's story would never be told. Your enthusiasm for the series and emails in my inbox keep me writing each new story in this universe.

Love and thanks to Cassandra V. She's my cheerleader, friend, and taskmaster. The shifters of Broken Peak thrived because of her support and encouragement.

Chan, she's a pillar of unconditional support and a reminder that I am not a complete and total hack when the insecurity hits and I spiral into the dreaded impostor syndrome.

I would be remiss in not thanking my friends and family, who put up with me during my seclusion in the writing cave and constantly offer their support and love.

Finally, and of course not least, the wonderful individuals who are responsible for the creation of the collector's edition of the Broken Peak Pack Omnibus: Kasey S., Sherry M., Meg M., Pyndan, Erin C., Rhel, Kieran, Rafael P, Sarah, and Melanie B. Little did they know that by supporting one little Kickstarter, they'd find a permanent spot on my acknowledgments page.

ABOUT THE AUTHOR

Jules Crisare loves writing sexy shifter romances. The growly and dominant males of Broken Peak and the Silver Sentinels are the ones bending to the strong wills of the smart heroines who cross their paths. Seriously, only strong heroines need apply to capture the hearts of these sexy alphas. Get your shifter loving fingers ready to turn those pages and explore the world of the Sentinels of the Silver Orb.

www.JCrisare.com

www.ingramcontent.com/pod-product-compliance
Lightning Source LLC
Chambersburg PA
CBHW051305210726
48287CB00002B/670